TRUE STORIES THAT MAKE THE MOST STEAMY SOAP OPERAS LOOK SQUEAKY CLEAN!

Listen to Dan Rather as he tries to defend himself against all the news that's fit to be whispered.

Sit in on the divorce case of *LA Law* star Harry Hamlin to see how the law game can really be played down and dirty.

Find out all the off-key-and-color things that Rose-anne Barr isn't singing out about.

Shudder at how brutal and bruising the battle of egos between Cybil Shepherd and Bruce Willis got when *Moonlighting* made ambitions howl.

Read the riveting blow-by-blow account of Joan Rivers' breakdown and fight to come back.

Learn how "outing" has exposed the lifestyles of stars who'd like to keep sexual proclivities undercover.

No lights are dimmed or punches pulled in the book that makes TV insiders squirm and TV viewers see TV shows and TV stars with an X-ray vision of the X-rated truth.

TV BABYLON II

TV BABYLON II

Jeff Rovin

A SIGNET BOOK

SIGNET
Published by the Penguin Group
Penguin Books USA Inc., 375 Hudson Street,
New York, New York 10014, U.S.A.
Penguin Books Ltd, 27 Wrights Lane,
London W8 5TZ, England
Penguin Books Australia Ltd, Ringwood,
Victoria, Australia
Penguin Books Canada Ltd, 10 Alcorn Avenue,
Toronto, Ontario, Canada M4V 3B2
Penguin Books (N.Z.) Ltd, 182–190 Wairau Road,
Auckland 10, New Zealand

Penguin Books Ltd, Registered Offices:
Harmondsworth, Middlesex, England

First published by Signet, an imprint of New American Library,
a division of Penguin Books USA Inc.

First Printing, August, 1991
10 9 8 7 6 5 4 3 2 1

Introduction

The world of TV Babylon, the world behind the cameras, has really outdone itself.

When the first edition of *TV Babylon* was published in 1984, it was filled with material culled from nearly forty years of television history. Although many of the stories were about contemporary stars—Mary Tyler Moore, John Belushi, and Joan Collins, for example—some of the most tragic tales were about TV celebrities of earlier generations, legends like George Reeves (*Superman*), Ernie Kovacs, and Dave Garroway.

Since the publication of the first book, something's happened in TV land: it's gotten even more unsavory and carnivorous. So much so that in just seven years, it's produced enough material for a second volume.

Some of this decay has been the fault of the stars themselves. Decades ago, if Lucy and Desi disagreed about how a scene should be played, they had the grace and good sense to settle it off to the side or privately with the director. Similarly, Sid Caesar and

Imogene Coca, Tony Randall and Jack Klugman, and many others.

For the most part, that kind of professionalism is gone. Dead. Egos as all-consuming as a black hole destroyed *Moonlighting*. They haunt *Roseanne*, have ravaged the once-mighty *Today* show, and threaten virtually every series in TV Babylon. There are still a few class acts in the business—Carol Burnett, *Designing Women*'s Dixie Carter, and Candice Bergen of *Murphy Brown* are outstanding examples. By and large, however, stars have become more tyrannical, drugged-out, and paranoid than ever.

There are several reasons for this.

Part of it is due to the ever-widening reach and power of the press, which deifies headliners and turns even the most ridiculously insignificant into major TV personalities. In the 1960s, it was a coup for a bona-fide star, let alone a costar, to make the cover of *TV Guide* or be featured in a major newspaper article. Today, anyone who appears on TV is considered newsworthy because there are so many media outlets eating up information. Not only do the so-called supermarket tabloids devote the bulk of their coverage to TV actors, but TV programs like *Entertainment Tonight* reach tens of millions of viewers *daily* (and, rather incongruously, make stars of *their* upbeat but uncharismatic hosts). Then there are *People* magazine, *Rolling Stone*, *Ladies' Home Journal*, the more gossipy-than-ever *TV Guide*, and other publications that make absolutely *sure* we know what Justine Bateman, Kirk Cameron, and Pat Sajak are wearing, eating, and thinking.

On the one hand, the attention feeds actors' egos. On the other hand, it makes many of them resentful and irrational: after an initial burst of publicity, most of them want their privacy, not press. (You should've gone into a different business, folks. Also, stop necking in restaurants if you don't want to be noticed.) In either case, it contributes to tension on the sets and in the home.

Another factor accelerating the decay of values in TV Babylon is money. That's nothing new, but in an era when videocassettes and cable are eating more and more into network audiences, eye-popping salaries are being pitched at stars who can hold an audience. If unprecedented fame doesn't warp an actor's perspectives, money usually does. And since the two tend to go hand-and-hand, the effect on the ego and temperament is multiplied.

Add one more ingredient to the stew and you have the new, unimproved TV Babylon: fear. In this, the actors are justified. The shooting of John Lennon wasn't a societal aberration. Other celebrities have been slain or attacked, and there's hardly a major or minor star in TV Babylon who hasn't a wacko or two trying to get *too* close. Delta Burke put it well: "Nowadays, I'm actually *relieved* when it's only a coyote in the bushes outside my house."

Johnny Carson notes that TV personalities are especially susceptible to being approached by fans. "If I'm out," he says, "there's nobody who doesn't feel free to come over to me. And no one ever calls me 'Mr. Carson.' It's, 'Hi, Johnny.' But if you're out to eat and you see Paul Newman, you don't go over. You point. Because Paul Newman is eight feet by ten feet. I'm twenty-one inches. You're comfortable with me. He's larger than life. He's a movie star, and therefore unreal."

Tragically, because of the pressures created by the new TV Babylon, preexisting problems have gotten worse than ever: infidelity, mental and physical abuse, suicide, and, of course, drug and alcohol addiction. Gregory Harrison, who costarred in *Trapper John, M.D.* and spent two years waging a ferocious battle against cocaine dependency says, "I got the trappings of success and it almost killed me. It's happened to almost everybody I've known who has had success."

As we said in the introduction to the first book, if you've only experienced TV from the outside, consider yourself fortunate. It's a place where the smiles are as false as a sitcom laugh track, the nightmares more attainable than the dreams, and the people richer than many, yet poorer than most.

Shooting Stars

Twenty-year-old Robert John Bardo of Tucson, Arizona, had three obsessions.

One was star Victoria Principal. At forty-six, the actress was beautiful and a mother figure, a woman of maturity and substance. But he'd read about Victoria, knew that her Beverly Hills home was a veritable fortress. In addition to bullet-proof windows, alarms, and attack dogs, there was a room like a bank vault—with a phone inside—in which the actress could hide from a would-be attacker.

She would be tough to get to.

Another obsession was vivacious teen rock star Debbie Gibson. Bardo listened to her records, watched her videos about teen love, and wrote to her. He wanted to visit her but she, too, seemed inaccessible. He had no idea where in New York she lived and, besides, she toured a great deal. He wasn't likely to meet her just by hanging around her home, even if he could find it. And he suspected that, like most rock stars, she'd have bodyguards most of the time.

Young, lovely Rebecca Schaeffer. (UPI/Bettmann)

Bardo's third and most consuming obsession was for another actress who had recently begun to make a splash in Hollywood. A perky, pretty twenty-one-year-old with a penchant for big, odd earrings and a glorious future ahead of her. A young woman named Rebecca Schaeffer.

A native of Eugene, Oregon, Rebecca had been a model until 1984, when she landed a role on the ABC soap opera *One Life to Live*. Parts in Woody Allen's *Radio Days* and on the NBC series *Amazing Stories* followed, after which she landed the role of Patti Russell, the younger sister of Pam Dawber's character Sam, on the TV series *My Sister Sam*. The show ran from 1986 to 1988, and though it was only a moderate success, there was talk of producing first-run episodes for syndication. Not that Rebecca needed the show: roles in the films *Scenes from the Class Struggle in*

Beverly Hills and *One Point of View* gave her additional serious acting credits, and she had just returned from Italy where she had a role in a TV miniseries about the 1985 hijacking of the Mediterranean cruise ship *Archille Lauro*.

Rebecca had everything . . . including an obsessed fan who was determined to meet her.

Bardo had written to Rebecca, and she'd obligingly sent him a publicity photo. Unlike the other two objects of his affection, he felt that she cared. Though he was nearly broke, that wouldn't matter to someone like Rebecca: he was handsome and devoted, and was convinced that if she met him she would love him.

He told his dreams to his sister, who tried to talk him out of chasing stars. She explained, as tactfully as possible, that they moved in different circles than Robert, that they had thousands of fans and wouldn't—couldn't—make time to see just one.

Robert told her that she was wrong. He said that he was going to prove it.

The young man knew that meeting Rebecca would not present a problem. She'd have to live somewhere around Los Angeles and, as a blossoming actress, wouldn't have the money to afford bodyguards or fancy security at her home. If he could find her, he'd be able to get close to her.

Packing a few possessions, Bardo headed west. As soon as he arrived in Los Angeles, he hired a private investigator to find out where Schaeffer lived. That proved easier than he'd expected: the Department of Motor Vehicles was only too happy to provide her home address.

Rebecca lived in a two-story apartment building in the Fairfax section of the city. On the morning of July

18, 1989, shortly after dawn, wearing a loose-fitting yellow shirt, Bardo boarded a bus and headed for her apartment building. He was carrying a large manila envelope stuffed with personal items, but two things most important of all. One was the cherished photo Rebecca had sent him. The other was a gun—just in case she spurned him. If he couldn't have her, no one would. It was that simple.

Upon arriving in the neighborhood, Bardo began walking back and forth along the street, in front of the apartment. His heart was drumming, and, for now, he simply wanted to savor being near her. As he paced, he looked at her door, at her dark windows, occasionally dragged a hand through his curly brown hair as he anxiously anticipated the long-awaited meeting. He *knew* she'd like him once she got to know him, but there was always the chance, however remote, that she wouldn't give him the time to explain, wouldn't understand the depth of his passion.

He was distracted when he saw a woman walking toward him. Purposefully, he walked toward her, his hand in the folder.

He took out the photo.

Though the young man knew which apartment was Rebecca's, he wanted to be reassured, to *hear* from someone who lived around here that the object of his affection was near. As he approached the woman, he held up the picture.

"Have you seen this girl in the neighborhood?" Bardo asked.

"*What?*" the woman asked, looking at him incredulously. Without stopping, she walked around the young man.

Ordinarily, her curt manner would have bothered

him. But he wouldn't give in to that—not now. It would ruin the day.

Bardo watched her go, then continued walking back and forth. He paced for nearly four hours, stopping other passersby, showing them the picture, asking if they knew the young woman. No one stopped to look or to talk to him. No one who saw the smoldering intensity in the young man's dark eyes felt that he had all his marbles. And, incredibly, no one called the police.

Finally, shortly after 10:00 A.M., Bardo had worked up the courage to go to the apartment. He walked quickly, stomach churning, and stopped at the door. He rang the doorbell, listened. He heard footsteps.

Rebecca opened the door, her pretty face looking up. Bardo smiled broadly as he reached into the folder and withdrew the picture.

He told Rebecca that she had sent this to him. He said that he was her biggest fan and that he wanted to talk to her.

Rebecca smiled nervously. As politely as possible, she said she was busy, then excused herself and started to shut the door.

Bardo was shocked. Angrily, reflexively, he put his foot against the door and shoved the photo back in the folder.

He had to be *important* to her, he'd told himself over and over as he'd walked. If not as her lover, then as the man who ended her life. He pulled out the gun.

When Rebecca saw the weapon, she stepped back. Bardo fired once, at her chest. Rebecca screamed as the bullet struck; a second, strangled cry escaped as the young woman fell.

Up and down the block, people looked out their

windows. Shoving the gun back into the envelope, Bardo turned from the apartment and ran toward the nearest bus stop. He felt no remorse: he couldn't have been kinder. She'd done this to herself.

The police and an ambulance arrived within minutes: less than a half hour after she was shot, Rebecca was pronounced dead at the Cedars-Sinai Medical Center.

Bardo headed back to Arizona, and during the long ride his mind, now, was tortured by thoughts of what he'd done, by the vision of Rebecca lying at his feet. He *didn't* feel that she belonged to him, as he'd expected; rather, the dominant emotions he felt now were shock and shame.

On the morning after the killing, a Tucson police officer approached Bardo as he ran through traffic. When the officer approached, the unkempt young man was muttering things about Rebecca and about the shooting; the officer took him to the police station. The police in Los Angeles were called, and detectives headed at once to Tucson to talk with him.

Bardo was charged with the murder of the actress and, in a hearing before Municipal Judge David Horwitz in Los Angeles, was ordered to stand trial for the crime. Because he had been "lying in wait," according to the courts, he faces death in the gas chamber if convicted. The trial began on December 7, 1990, with Bardo's attorney, Steven Galindo, noting that Bardo is under constant medication but was improving mentally—for which the world is grateful.

As horrified as people were by the violent crime itself, those emotions paled beside the shock of how easy it had been for Bardo to get Rebecca's address from the Department of Motor Vehicles. As a result of the killing, the California legislature quickly passed,

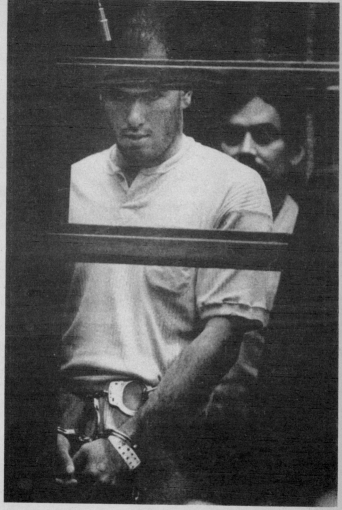

Robert John Bardo in custody. (UPI/Bettman)

and Governor Deukmejian signed, a law written by
Assemblyman Michael Roos of Los Angeles. It stipu-
lates that any organization that wants information
from the DMV must post a $50,000 bond as well as a
$250 application fee every two years. Governor Deuk-
mejian also ordered that DMV wait ten days before
releasing such information, and that they inform the
subject exactly who is requesting it.

"This was precipitated by a personal tragedy beyond
belief," Roos says, adding, "We intend to prevent this
tragedy from ever happening again."

It's tragic indeed that a young woman who came to
Hollywood to win recognition as an actress will be best
remembered for what has been dubbed "the Schaeffer
law."

Sadly, it's the kind of immortality TV Babylon
grants with shameful regularity.

A Hope of Ray

It's rare that obsessed fans make it to a star's home, as Robert John Bardo did. It's even rarer when they make it inside. But it *does* happen.

Sometimes the results are annoying but only potentially dangerous, as in the case of thirty-seven-year-old Margaret Ray of Crawford, Colorado. In May of 1988, Ray pulled up to a toll booth at the Lincoln Tunnel in New York City. Unable to pay it, she announced that she was Mrs. David Letterman, and that her son was David Letterman, Jr. She said she'd send them the money.

The woman was arrested, not because she was lying about her identity, but because the car she was driving, a Porsche, had been reported stolen from Letterman's home in affluent New Canaan, Connecticut.

Letterman declined to press charges. He was just glad to have the car back and the culprit identified, figuring that was the end of "Mrs. Letterman."

Little did he know—

David Letterman in his marshmallow suit, being cooked by members of the studio audience. Offscreen, he was taking heat as well. (AP/Wide World)

Later describing the late night TV host as "the dominant figure in my life," Ray returned to Letterman's home, intent on setting up housekeeping. She was arrested and charged with trespassing, but was once again released when she promised never to bother Letterman again.

Ray stayed away until February 24 of the following

year, when she went back to the house, was arrested, and again released. She came back four days later. This time she was arrested and sentenced to three years' probation, all of it to be served in Colorado, far from Letterman.

But Ms. Ray had other plans. She headed east and, on August 24, went back to Letterman's house for a *fifth* time. Now the courts had had enough. Ray was arrested and sentenced the very next day to nine months in prison for violating her probation. Ray did seven months at the Niantic State Prison for Women in Niantic, Connecticut, and was released on Friday, March 16.

On Sunday, March 18, she went back to Letterman's home, broke a window, and entered. Letterman was upstairs at the time. Going to investigate, he came face to face with Ray and called the police. She was removed from the property and warned not to return.

To no one's surprise, the woman came back the next morning. Letterman found her in the hallway and phoned the police, then walked over to Ms. Ray and told her he'd placed the call. Calmly, the woman nodded and said she'd wait outside. When the police arrived, they found Ray near the tennis court. Held on $1,000 bond, the woman was taken to Norwalk Superior Court where she was ordered to undergo a psychiatric evaluation. In the meantime, it was back to Niantic State Prison.

The next night, Letterman opened his show by calling his home and letting the phone ring eight times . . . just to make sure no one was there.

On April 30, the saga came to an end—for now—when Letterman told Norwalk Superior Court Judge

Lawrence L. Hauser that Ray *wasn't* his wife, and that, "When she broke into my home, that is the first time I discovered she was on this planet."

Ray was sent to Fairfield Hills Hospital in Newton, Connecticut. However, in March of the following year, she fled the psychiatric institution, leaving a note that said she was going home to Colorado and would never again bother the late night star.

Will she ever go back to the house on North Wilton Road?

Stay tuned. No doubt David Letterman will.

Penn Pal

Letterman's "wife" was never armed, but if she *had* been, the scenario might have been similar to what happened on March 30 in the home of Emmy-winning *Cagney and Lacey* star Sharon Gless.

Back in 1986, short, stocky Joni Leigh Penn, then twenty-eight, began sending letters to the forty-four-year-old actress. A lesbian and aspiring actress, the Garden Grove, California, fan wrote 100 letters in all, but didn't stop there. At the Emmy Awards ceremony in 1988, she tried to get close to Gless in order to give her two long-stemmed roses. Unable to get past security personnel, Penn tried to think of some other way to meet Gless.

Gless first became concerned about Penn's activities in August of that year, after Penn's psychiatrist contacted *Cagney and Lacey* producer Barry Rosenzweig and told him that his patient had threatened to kill herself in the presence of Gless. The producer informed Gless, who immediately contacted police to ask for a restraining order, noting in part, "I've been told that the intention is not to harm me, but to harm herself in front of me. But . . . these people get very confused. They don't know if you are them. They start to blend with you."

On October 25, before officials had gotten around to acting on the matter, Penn rendered the question moot. She went to Gless's one-story stucco home at the end of a shady cul-de-sac in Studio City, slipped around the sliding gate, and rang the doorbell. Gless's secretary came out, and Penn calmly announced that she had a gun and was going to use it on herself. The secretary didn't know whether or not to believe Penn, and didn't get to find out: no sooner had the disturbed caller made her pronouncement then she fled.

In November, bolstered by a letter from Penn's psychiatrist, a Superior Court judge finally ordered Penn to stay away from the actress, her home, and her relatives, and Penn did so for nearly half a year. But the temptation to go back was great, and eventually Penn succumbed. When she returned to Gless's house at three in the morning on Friday, March 30, 1990, there was no doubt about her intentions. Dressed in blue jeans and a billowing green shirt, carrying a duffel bag and armed with an AT-22 assault rifle and 500 rounds of ammunition, she boldly entered the house looking for Gless. There was now a new wrinkle in her scheme: though she still intended to turn the rifle on herself, she planned to do so after sexually assaulting the actress.

But it turned out that no one was home, and as Penn made her way through the empty house she became more and more frustrated. Meanwhile, as soon as Penn had entered the house, an alarm had gone off at the police station and officers rushed over. When they entered, they confronted Penn who began shouting incoherently. When they made a move toward her, she pointed the gun at herself.

"I'll use it!" she shouted. "Don't touch me, I'll use it!"

The officers stopped: in her frantic state they weren't sure what Penn would do. And as one of the officers later put it, with the rifle she was carrying, "She could have turned anyone within range into hamburger."

As they watched, the young woman backed into a bathroom and locked the door. The officers stood back: if Penn fired through the door, she'd still be able to cut any of them down.

A SWAT team was summoned and, after ten residences around Gless's had been evacuated, they entered the home.

They approached the bathroom, where they could hear Penn muttering to herself. An officer experienced in hostage negotiations began speaking with her, but Penn cut him off, resentful of the fact a man had been sent to the house. Officer Patricia Stark was rushed over from police headquarters.

For several hours Stark stood beside the door, talking to the disturbed young woman. Penn alternately raved about how she was going to kill herself and cried about how much she loved Gless and wanted to meet her. Stark lent a sympathetic ear, and over the next few hours was able to calm the disturbed young woman and win her trust.

Finally, seven hours later, the exhausted Penn put down her gun and surrendered to police. Silent, her expression blank, she was handcuffed and led to a waiting squad car.

"She was tired," Captain Dan Watson told reporters later. "She was just kind of worn down."

Penn was charged with two counts of burglary, bail was set at $500,000, and Penn was held for psychiatric tests at the Sybil Brand Institute. Six weeks later, at a preliminary hearing in San Fernando Municipal Court, Gless testified that she had not been terribly alarmed by Penn's letters because they were not threatening, and, "I didn't think something like this would ever happen, never in a million years."

In July of 1990, Joni Leigh Penn pleaded no contest to two felony burglary charges in San Fernando Superior Court and was sentenced to six years in prison. She would be eligible for parole after three years, four months.

An interesting sidebar to the story—and a concise commentary on the sad condition of Penn's mind—is what was found inside her duffel bag. In addition to a jeans jacket and a rifle cleaning kit, there were two books: *Acting: The First Lessons,* and Tennessee Williams's *The Glass Menagerie.* A curious, paradoxical mix, yet a fitting tribute to TV Babylon, a place that is part artistry, part insanity.

Talk Showdowns

For the moment, David Letterman and Sharon Gless can put their security worries behind them. But they're far from being the only stars whose lives have been haunted by obsessive or deranged fans. In fact, two other talk-show hosts were stalked by people decidedly more deadly than Letterman's "wife."

Arsenio Hall has been the target of a number of threats and plots, ranging from local gang leaders who disapprove of the fact that he's dated singer Paula Abdul, who is not black (or maybe they're just damn jealous), to a limousine driver who arrived to pick up Hall—then hightailed it from the studio when the comedian's *real* driver showed up.

It's bad enough that Hall has to endure these crazies, but it's worse when his audience gets caught in the maelstrom. Nine times during the last six months of 1989, a caller phoned the Paramount studios where *The Arsenio Hall Show* is taped and said there was a bomb in the auditorium. The first eight times the mystery terrorist called was before audiences arrived for taping. The studio was searched on each occasion, and nothing was found. Then, in December, the terrorist phoned during the taping itself.

Head of security Tom Hays says, "When a situation like this does arise, we have to think things like, 'Do we evacuate?' " In this case they didn't. Only Arsenio was informed of the potential danger and the show went on as security forces, most of them plainclothes, snooped around the studio. But, Hays says, though the caller has thus far been bluffing, he's worried that "The day we say, 'It's just him again,' that could be the day the whole stage blows up."

Arsenio's nemesis has been nameless and faceless. In contrast, the man who was out to get Hall's professional rival, Johnny Carson, made his name and likeness unnervingly familiar.

Not content with drafting hate mail to then-President Reagan, thirty-six-year-old former mental patient Kenneth Orville Gause of Milwaukee, Wisconsin, turned his sights on Carson. He first contacted the late-night host in 1987, using two different means of communication: letters, which he signed with his real name followed by "the Baron KOG" and a skull and crossbones; and a chilling videotape, in which Gause—a 240-pound black man—pretended to be the natty Carson interviewing a nonexistent guest.

During the next two years there were five communications in all, in which Gause, an aspiring entertainer and filmmaker, claimed to have sent songs and skit ideas to Carson, which Johnny allegedly stole. Then, in August of 1989, Gause started playing psychotic hardball: he said that if he wasn't paid $5 million at once, he'd blow up the studio.

Gause waited until November, and when the money didn't arrive he wrote to Carson and said that he was coming out. Additional security was hired at the Burbank studio, and pictures of Gause were left at all the entrances. An accompanying bulletin read, "Do not admit for any reason. Contact security immediately if seen."

True to his word, during the last week of November, Gause boarded a bus in Milwaukee and headed to southern California. At first, on November 28, he tried to see Carson at the star's home in Malibu. But the star had hired off-duty police to watch the place, and Gause realized he wouldn't be able to get in. Returning to downtown L.A., he caught a cab and went to the studio. Armed with a billy club and a sock full of gravel, he entered the lobby and yelled, "I have to see Johnny *now*!" While the guard phoned for assistance, Gause stormed into the studio, searching for Carson's office. The police, too, were summoned.

Additional guards arrived quickly and, telling Carson to stay in his office, they went after the intruder. Ranting and shouting, Gause wasn't difficult to find. Gun drawn, a guard ordered him to stop; Gause did so.

"Johnny's got my money, and I want to *get* it," he said.

The guard replied, "Don't move."

Another guard stepped over and took away the bludgeon. Gause continued to complain about Carson, but he remained where he was standing until police arrived. They booked him for making terrorist threats, attempted extortion, and carrying a concealed weapon. Bail was set at a quarter of a million dollars.

Interviewed in prison by Milwaukee TV station

WVTV, Gause was lucid and sincere. And, clearly, very, very demented. "I tried to talk Johnny Carson into releasing the remainder of my money that he hasn't spent or gambled off and to let me have the keys to the warehouse where they keep my money and my presents." Gause also noted that he gets more fan mail than Carson, Michael J. Fox, and Michael Jackson combined.

Gause was arraigned in Pasadena Superior Court on February 2, 1990. He pleaded guilty to ten felony counts of mailing extortion letters and making threats. Judge Charles Lee sentenced him to five years' probation and ordered him home to Milwaukee to undergo psychiatric treatment. Gause was also barred from contacting Carson in the future.

Geeks Bearing Gifts

It's amazing and not a little disconcerting how little the courts can do to protect celebrities. For instance, over a two-year period, twenty-seven-year-old Tina Marie Ledbetter sent *Family Ties* star Michael J. Fox six *thousand* letters—eight hundred of which she mailed the month he wed actress Tracy Pollan. In the early notes, she expressed her affection for Fox; in the later ones, she told the actor how deeply she disapproved of his marriage to Pollan.

But disapproval isn't a warning or a threat, and the authorities could do nothing. Only when Ledbetter began writing letters suggesting that harm would come to the couple and their newborn son, Sam, was she arrested and charged with making terrorist threats. In December of 1989, Ledbetter pleaded guilty to three counts of felony: after agreeing to seek psychiatric help, she was given three years' probation; no jail time.

Ledbetter may reform, but chances are good the

Fox family won't be holding its breath. They'll be watching and waiting in case she or some other devoted "fan" decides to become involved in their lives.

Although the threats against male stars are chilling, the preponderance of fanatics go after the young, attractive females. Sometimes the incidents are isolated and impulsive, as in 1988 when a man spotted beautiful Tracy Scoggins of *The Colbys* in a hotel elevator and simply reached out and ripped her dress off. Whatever else might have happened was cut short by the actress's screams, and the attacker was nabbed by hotel workers. He was arrested and charged with misdemeanor sexual assault.

More often than not, though, the pursuit of females is an ongoing affair. For several weeks, a fan sent *Newhart*'s Mary Frann roses and mail. She thought it was innocent infatuation until he sent her a $12,000 diamond bracelet with a message: "We will be meeting very soon. When you least expect it, I will be there."

Alarmed, Frann notified police, who—surprise!—couldn't do anything because there was no implicit threat. Frann has not heard from her admirer since, and, like the Foxes, can do nothing but wait.

Similarly, Mary Hart, former Miss South Dakota and chirpy cohost of the daily syndicated series *Entertainment Tonight*. The thirty-eight-year-old (whose legs, incidentally, are considered such an asset that they've been insured for $2 million) has been the object of not one but two men's affections in 1989 alone: a psychiatric patient in Illinois wrote, expressing his intention to visit her upon his release, and a Kansas man with a police record not only phoned repeatedly but came to the Paramount lot where the show is taped. Luckily, a mug shot had been given to guards and they stopped him from entering—though he *was* able to get away and is still at large.

Also on the loose is the Vietnam veteran who posed as a surveyor, went to the Coldwater Canyon home of *L.A. Law* star Susan Dey, and tried to get in to see her. He fled only when a housekeeper phoned police.

Compared to "the ones that got away," the numbers of lunatics who are caught and put away remain naggingly slim.

Warren Sevy Hudson, an admirer of popular KNBC-TV (Los Angeles) news anchorwoman Kelly Lange, went from sending her little presents to threatening to blow her brains out—typical of the "if-I-can't-have-you-no-one-will" school of madmen. Hudson was arrested and convicted. Ohio janitor Richard Pelfrey, a "Vannatic" intent on marrying *Wheel of Fortune* hostess Vanna White, phoned repeatedly, and then was court-ordered to stay a minimum of 150 feet away from her after leaping up from the audience and trying to reach the letter-turner during a taping. (Turns out that Pelfrey was two-timing her, however: at the same time he was "courting" Vanna, he was also pursuing teenage rock star Debbie Gibson. Debbie seems to have lucked out in the lunatic-fan department.)

A more uncommon but no less dangerous situation was that faced by fourteen-year-old Danny Pintauro of *Who's the Boss*. He was the recipient of "graphically sexual" letters sent by a gay admirer, twenty-eight-year-old Mark Budman, of Carson, California. Danny's mother, Peggy, intercepted the letters and contacted authorities; on June 7, 1990, Budman was charged with two misdemeanor counts of sending "bizarre letters featuring sexual acts." He was scheduled to appear in court five days later: when he didn't show, authorities learned that he'd been taken to Harbor-UCLA Medical Center on June 8, after having poured a quart of the pesticide malathion down his throat. Budman, who was also suffering from AIDS, died eleven days later.

Yet, of all the stories of TV stars being stalked by unwanted suitors, one of the most unnerving was the case of Stephanie Zimbalist, daughter of TV actor Efrem Zimbalist, Jr., and the star of numerous TV movies and the long-running series *Remington Steele*.

Beginning in August of 1988, the then-thirty-two-year-old star began receiving fan mail from someone who signed the letters simply, "Your Secret Admirer." Shortly thereafter, the letters started arriving at her home. And when she did a play on the road, her admirer wrote and recounted specifics about each performance. *That* made her really nervous. He also wrote to Stephanie's friends and colleagues, introducing himself to them . . . as though he were in her life to stay. Later, she learned that he'd been closer to her than just a front-row seat: he'd actually gotten backstage on various occasions, by pretending to be everyone from a technician to her brother Efrem Zimbalist III. Unknown to her at the time, he'd also made a pilgrimage to the camp and boarding school she'd attended as a child, just to be closer to where she'd been.

The letters continued coming, with passages like, "I want to see you. I want to hear you. I want to be near you. Your various retainers aren't going to stop me." Yet, there were still no actionable threats, and no name attached to any of them. Then the twisted pen pal got even bolder. In December of 1989, he wrote, "I am watching your house," and enclosed a photo he'd taken of Stephanie's Woodland Hills, California, home to prove it. He also said, "I want the police to watch me. I want them to get used to me. I want them to get bored." The implication was clear: when they let down their guard, he'd make his move.

All of this was unnerving enough, but things got

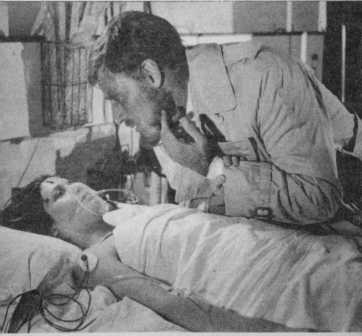

Stephanie Zimbalist playing the part of a seriously ill young woman . . . a role that very nearly came true for her. (© Orion Pictures)

even dicier the following February, when Stephanie took to the stage in Pasadena with the play *The Baby Dance*. Her correspondent wrote and said that he was coming to Los Angeles, and that she would suffer if she did the show. The actress was torn: as in foreign policy, it's a bad idea to give in to terrorist threats. But the man *had* been following her for more than a year, he might not be bluffing. Reluctantly, Stephanie canceled several performances.

Then, at last, the actress had a stroke of good luck. The star-struck sickie wrote and said that he was coming to see her. He told her when he'd arrive in L.A., and what plane he'd be on. He also listed the other flights he'd taken to be in the audience at her performances.

And, after writing, "Don't say I didn't warn you," finally he signed his name.

FBI agents looked up the passenger lists of the flights he'd listed. Everything checked out and, on March 2, 1990, they went to the airport to meet his plane. With the help of airline officials, they found out which passenger was their quarry and followed the heavyset man to a hotel in Sherman Oaks—less than two miles from Stephanie's home. There, they arrested forty-two-year-old Michael Lawrence Shields, an unemployed native of Plymouth, Michigan. He was charged with violating the "extortion statute," a federal crime, and was hauled off to prison. Shields himself requested that bail be denied, since it would put his mother under severe hardship to pay it. Los Angeles Federal Magistrate Joseph Reichmann was happy to comply, noting wryly, "It's not often I get to give a defendant exactly what he wants."

In August of 1990, Shields pleaded guilty to seven

counts of mailing threatening communications; it was a plea bargain that was supposed to guarantee him no more than a year in prison. (Why did the prosecutor's office settle for such a relatively mild sentence? As Assistant U.S. Attorney Carol Gillam noted, there *were*, after all, no outright threats in the letters.) However, prosecutors later came back with testimony from a psychiatrist who said that Shields suffers from a borderline personality disorder that may be untreatable. The judge rejected the plea bargain, declaring that "the pervasive, repetitive stalking of the victim would compel one to conclude that the plea agreement was too generous." Instead, U.S. District Judge John G. Davies ordered him to serve two years in prison and three on probation. He was forbidden from approaching or communicating with twenty-six people, including Zimbalist and her father.

What can Zimbalist expect when Shields gets out? According to Dr. Park Dietz, who had studied John Hinckley after the man's attack on President Reagan, Shields exhibits many of the characteristics of people who are prone to attack public figures. Like Michael J. Fox and the others, all Zimbalist can do is keep her fingers crossed.

In commenting on the apprehension of Shields, FBI special agent Lawrence G. Lawler said, "By this arrest, we intend to serve notice that this sort of criminal activity will be investigated and prosecuted with all vigor."

Mr. Lawler is, perhaps, a tad optimistic if he thinks that the wackos who fly around the country chasing stars are going to be dissuaded by Shields's arrest. (Indeed, because Shields was examined by a prosecution psychiatrist without the issuing of a court order, a motion was filed by the defense to have the charges dismissed. U.S. District Judge John Davies declined, although he forbade prosecutors from utilizing the psychiatric evaluation. What signal does *this* send to the loons out in TV Babylon? That there are all kinds of loopholes they can crawl through.)

In light of all this, comedian and talk-show host Joan Rivers is taking a different, seemingly more practical approach to the problem of security. In July of 1990, Rivers went to police headquarters in New York City and got herself a gun permit. Captain Allan Shulman of the License Bureau said, "I was waiting for something to make me laugh, but she was serious."

Dead serious, you might say.

Missing Kitty

From 1955 to 1975, Amanda Blake played the strong, worldly, compassionate Kitty Russell, aka Miss Kitty, on the series *Gunsmoke*. In real life, Amanda was just as strong, and even more giving. She had her moods—she was married five times—but her generosity with time and money was unparalleled. She was particularly devoted to animals: after *Gunsmoke* was canceled, Amanda would go to Africa whenever possible, studying animals and learning more about preservation efforts. In her later years, the actress lived outside of Sacramento with Pat Derby and Ed Stewart, owners of a twenty-acre "retirement home" for show business animals, and virtually all her free time was devoted to their charity PAWS (Performing Animal Welfare Society).

After one trip to Africa late in 1988, Pat recalls that Amanda "looked awful and was really sick. We thought it was the flu." But the truth was far, far worse. Amanda had felt weak for months and, on a

Amanda Blake, with James Arness, in happier days on the set of *Gunsmoke*. (Howard Frank Collection)

previous stay in Africa, she'd gone to see a doctor
who told her that she had AIDS. Amanda had contracted the disease from her late husband, Mark
Spaeth, whom she had married in 1984 and divorced
less than a year later. Not long after that, the bisexual
Spaeth had died of the disease.

Though Amanda told at least one person, her
housekeeper, that the marriage had never been con-
summated, she was lying; in truth, the relationship
came apart after she learned that Spaeth had the disease . . . and, incredibly, had known about it two
months before they got married.

Amanda kept her illness a secret from even her closest friends. It wasn't until she returned from the Afri-
can trip, looking ill, that Pat went to a local doctor
with her and they learned the truth: tests confirmed
that she had AIDS. With Pat and Ed in the room, the
doctor talked to Amanda about things she needed to
do to help control the disease.

"We were shocked," Pat says. "It was the first we'd
heard."

While the doctor talked, Amanda just stared blankly
at a wall; not once did she look at her friends. Pat
says that they never talked about it after they left the
office, either.

"She wasn't bitter and she wasn't angry. That was
just the way she wanted it, and we respected it." Pat
adds that Amanda wanted to keep it a secret so that
her life wouldn't turn into a "goldfish bowl."

Though Amanda took AZT, the disease worked its
evil quickly: in July, less than a year after that visit
to the American doctor, the sixty-year-old actress
entered Mercy General Hospital. She died there on
August 16, 1989. In accordance with her wishes, the

hospital and her friends said that the actress had died from a recurrence of oral cancer. The truth only became known due to an unfortunate turn of events.

Three days before her death, Amanda had changed her will to leave PAWS her entire estate, which consisted largely of the $400,000 house Amanda had left empty when she went to live with Pat and Ed. Spearheaded by a sister and two cousins (with whom Amanda had had no contact for years), the family attempted to contest the will, filing a suit which claimed that Amanda was suffering from "head and neck cancer" and, thus, "was not of sound and disposing mind." After deep soul-searching, Pat decided to tell the truth so that Amanda's reputation and integrity would not be dirtied. She wanted people to understand that Amanda had been gravely ill, but not mentally unfit. As Pat succinctly put it, "Amanda didn't care about [her family] and they never cared anything about her. Amanda cared about animals."

In light of some of the people she knew, who can blame her?

The court did not alter the bequest, and as a last, touching tribute to the actress, the elephant habitat at the PAWS compound was named Lake Amanda.

It's the kind of immortality she'd have cherished.

Ill Street

Although the AIDS-related death of actor Rock Hudson did a great deal to bring the disease out into the open, many celebrity victims still won't admit when they're afflicted with the disease. For however long it drags on, many won't be able to get work; insurance companies are reluctant to underwrite projects that may have to be reshot due to the incapacitation or death of an actor. Then there's the public to consider: only the very bravest souls will risk spending the remainder of their days being treated as lepers. It's a sad commentary on the state of human compassion but, for the present, it's an inescapable fact. So the roster of celebrities who smile on the outside while they die on the inside continues to swell.

There *are* exceptions. Franklyn Seales—Dexter Stuffins on *Silver Spoons*—had never been secretive about being gay. When he became ill, he told friends that he had AIDS; they were there for him in the spring of 1990 when he fought the last leg of his battle against the disease. Franklyn was relatively fortunate: he'd also been given a recurring role on *Amen*, as Lorenzo Hollingsworth. The part was there for him whenever he was up to working. But Franklyn was a *rare* exception.

One TV star who was sick with AIDS and kept it a secret from family as well as friends and fans was

Rock Hudson and Susan St. James on the set of *McMillan and Wife* in 1973. In 1975, Ms. St. James was written out of the series in a plane crash, and Mr. Hudson continued alone. In real life, the actor endured a far greater tragedy. (Howard Frank Collection)

Rene Enriquez, who played the chronically worried Lt. Ray Calletano on *Hill Street Blues*. Enriquez was the third cast member to die: Trinidad Silva (Jesus Martinez) was struck and killed by a drunk driver, and Michael Conrad (Sgt. Phil Esterhaus) died of cancer. However, Enriquez's death was in many ways the saddest.

Enriquez belonged to a distinguished Nicaraguan family. His uncle, Emiliano Chamorro, was president of the nation prior to the Somoza regime; many other family members were and remain politically active. Naturally, no one was thrilled when Enriquez announced that he wanted to become an actor instead of a politician. But he came to the United States and followed his dream and, in time, earned a reputation as a solid film and TV actor, the latter through roles in shows such as *Quincy* and *Police Story*. In his five seasons on *Hill Street Blues*, he did a great deal to boost the self-image of Hispanics, particularly in the 1982 episode in which he gave a moving speech about discrimination.

Partly because he was a role model for Hispanics, and partly because his Roman Catholic family would have been horrified, Enriquez kept his gay liftstyle a deep secret. Whenever he went to parties or industry functions, he would bring a woman. Although his gay, Hispanic housemate also accompanied them, Enriquez always introduced him as his assistant. In conversation, the actor would talk about a wife who had died (he'd never been married) and, in 1987, when he learned that he had AIDS, he told associates it was pancreatic cancer. Only his two sisters and his lover knew the truth.

But even though Enriquez didn't work much, he

didn't just lie down and die. He was devoted to children, and not only did he found an orphanage in Mexico and contribute to several others, he used his contacts to arrange celebrity tennis tournaments to raise money for the facilities. He also gave time and money to the National Hispanic Arts Endowment.

When the fifty-six-year-old actor died on March 23, 1990, his sisters had his body quickly cremated in an effort to keep the cause of death secret, and spare his family profound mortification. The death certificate told the true story, however: cytomegalovirus enteritis due to Acquired Immune Deficiency Syndrome.

His family was shocked and outraged, and close friends and coworkers were hurt and disappointed that Enriquez hadn't told them the truth. But that will fade in time, and Rene Enriquez's testament will be the truths he spoke on *Hill Street Blues*, and what he did with his last remaining months.

A Celebrity Cause

In 1975, actor Paul Michael Glaser began a four-year-long run on the police show *Starsky and Hutch*, capping a long climb to the top, which began with parts in feature films and in TV series like *The Waltons*, *Toma*, and various soap operas. When the show was canceled, he undertook a career as a director of TV and feature movies—having helmed several episodes of *Starsky and Hutch*—and also starred in TV films like *The Great Houdini* and *Princess Daisy*.

Despite a prosperous career, his greatest joy came from his wife, Elizabeth Glaser, five years his junior, who was a director of exhibits for the Los Angeles Children's Museum. And in 1981, the couple eagerly looked forward to the birth of their first child. But instead of bringing them joy, the event propelled them into unthinkable despair.

In her ninth month of pregnancy, Elizabeth began bleeding heavily and was taken to the Cedars-Sinai Medical Center. Although doctors were able to deliver the baby, Elizabeth required transfusions totaling seven pints of blood before the hemorrhaging stopped.

Four years later, the Glasers had an active young daughter, Ariel, a one-and-one-half-year-old son, Jake, and a good life. Then, Ariel became increasingly lethargic and was constantly getting sick. Doctors couldn't find anything wrong with her and, casting their net wider, decided to test her for AIDS.

The results were positive. And as each member of the family was tested, the news got worse. Elizabeth tested HIV positive, as did Jake. Elizabeth had contracted the disease during the transfusions and had unwittingly passed it on to her daughter during eight months of breast feeding. Jake had contracted it in the womb. Only Paul tested negative.

Numbing as the news was, once the Glasers got over the initial shock, they decided to go public with the story. As Glaser explains it, "Our family situation shows how hard it is to get the disease. Until we found out our family was infected, Elizabeth and I had a natural sexual relationship." He adds that the kids "bled on me, they crapped on me, they hugged me and they kissed me. And I still don't have it."

Despite that fact, when the Glasers told their friends, many pulled away, and others refused to let their children play with Ariel and Jake. Expecting the worst, the couple told the directors of Crossroads, a private school to which Ariel had just been accepted, that the girl had AIDS. The administrators couldn't have been more compassionate: they reassured the Glasers that the invitation to attend still stood. She began classes in the fall of 1986.

In the summer of 1987, Ariel weakened noticeably, and couldn't attend school that September. Crossroads

The Glasers on Capitol Hill, asking the House Budget Committee's Task Force on Human Resources to provide more money for pediatric AIDS research. (AP/Wide World)

made certain that a tutor visited the home three times a week to give her lessons. Incredibly, even as the disease ravaged the child, her doctor wasn't allowed to give her AZT: the only known AIDS treatment had not been approved for children.

By 1988, the girl could barely walk or talk, and her

parents had to feed her—solid foods eventually giving way to IVs, which the Glasers administered themselves. She was admitted to the hospital in April of 1988—where, even though it was too late, she was finally allowed to have AZT. Ariel fought to survive, but she succumbed on August 12, a few days after her seventh birthday.

Years of preparation didn't make the inevitable any easier, but Paul and Elizabeth refused to sink into despair. Elizabeth recalls thinking at the time, "There is something wrong in the world that research isn't being handled with the speed and care that it needs." She intended to do something about that.

Paul's fame as a TV star had brought national attention to the case and, using that attention, Elizabeth worked hard to raise funds for pediatric AIDS research. Traveling to Washington, she helped convince Congress to up the research budget from $3.3 million to nearly three times that, and to open new treatment facilities. Dissatisfied still, Elizabeth and two friends established the Pediatric AIDS Foundation to raise more money; within a year of Ariel's death, Elizabeth had collected more than $2.5 million, which was parceled out in the form of grants.

The Foundation, which started in a tiny spare bedroom, now has its own office in Santa Monica, California, and is doing more for the problem than the monolithic U.S. government.

Elizabeth has been taking AZT since 1988, and realizes that both she and her son are medical time bombs. However, the Glasers believe that the lesson of their story is one of hope, not despondency. It is, says Paul, "A story about how we rise above our fears, how we all have to be stronger than we ever thought we could be."

A story which, thanks to the Glasers, may end happily for thousands of children across the country.

The Cast Is Stoned

In 1987, history was made. It was the first time an animated character was brought down by alleged drug abuse.

The show was *Mighty Mouse: The New Adventures*, and with a cry of "Here I come to save the day!" one misguided but very vocal leader of a watchdog group was convinced, beyond a doubt, that when the superhero paused to sniff a flower and was revitalized, it was cocaine he was snorting. The fellow's interpretation was reinforced (or more likely brought on) by the fact that the series was the work of Ralph Bakshi, the animator who had directed the X-rated feature-length cartoon *Fritz the Cat* fifteen years before.

Though Bakshi articulately and energetically denied the allegation, the charge was picked up by the media, the damage was done, and the image-conscious (and boycott-wary) CBS canned the show.

No one denies that use of cocaine is widespread in TV Babylon, and that the ability to provide the drug often determines who gets jobs behind the cameras. On a network series that aired in the middle 1980s, one production company employee quit because he was overlooked, repeatedly, for promotions and raises. Not-so-coincidentally, he was practically the only staff member who didn't supply the producer with cocaine.

On another program, *The Pat Sajak Show*, one technician was arrested in March of 1990 after a three-week police undercover operation revealed that he was selling cocaine. Other technicians were suspected to be part of the arrested man's ring of cocaine users and/or sellers and, although there were some two-week suspensions, nothing was ever proven.

The staffs and stars of TV shows will always abuse one substance or another. In our previous volume, *TV Babylon*, we recounted the bottle-battles of such stars as Sid Caesar, Daniel J. Travanti, and Dick Van Dyke. Others have struggled against the grip of alcohol as well. Kenneth Charles Swofford, who played Frank Flannigan on *The Adventures of Ellery Queen* (1975) and principal Quentin Morloch on *Fame* (1983–1985) had more than just a liquor problem after he went driving drunk. On December 17, 1989, he went directly from a bar to his car and drove right into another vehicle, causing serious injury to a man and his two young sons. Swofford pleaded no contest to felony drunk driving, and was handed a prison sentence of twenty-eight months and ordered to pay nearly $10,000 in restitution to the family. He subsequently sought help from Alcoholics Anonymous.

A few months later, on February 23, actor Jeff Conaway, who starred as Bobby Wheeler on *Taxi* (1978–1981) and as Prince Erik Greystone on *Wizards and Warriors* (1983), hopped into his sports car and also went driving drunk. Tearing down a street in Los Angeles, he hit a young bicyclist, breaking his leg and ripping open the man's scalp. Conaway's blood alcohol content was .15—nearly double the state limit for legal intoxication. The repentant actor did not go to prison.

The highest-profile actor who suffered from a problem with alcohol is something of a surprise: clean-cut, athletic David Hasselhoff, star of *Knight Rider* (1982–1986) and *Baywatch* (1989).

While most actors who fall into a bottle do so because of career problems (it's cheaper than cocaine and, after all, they aren't working), Hasselhoff got into trouble after the collapse of his marriage to actress Catherine Hickland in 1987.

"I traveled the world, mostly out of my head," he says. "I played at Ernest Hemingway for that whole time." He says he went on "a complete binge," not only boozing it up but crawling into bed with woman after woman. "Sometimes it wasn't the nicest-looking women," he admits, but he wasn't being picky. He just didn't want to be alone.

Upon his return in August of 1989, he started the series *Baywatch* and cleaned himself up with the help of actress Pamela Bach, who had a bit part in an episode of the series. The two fell in love and were wed in December of 1989.

Young Goners

The sudden fame and money—or loss of same—which sends many Babylonians in a drug or alcohol tailspin is unfortunate and heartbreaking. Yet, it isn't as distressing as the effect TV Babylon has on the young and innocent—not just the kids who become famous and can't handle it, but the children who live in the shadow of fame, the sons and daughters of the stars.

Sometimes it's an inferiority complex that drives them to drugs and drink. Sometimes it's the neglect that comes from having a parent or parents who work long hours. Sometimes it's just the corrupt environment of TV Babylon that does them in. Occasionally, it's all of the above.

Though the deaths of the children of motion picture stars such as Gregory Peck, Paul Newman, and Jill Ireland have dominated the press, TV stars have had their share of grief as well. The drug bouts of the daughters of Carol Burnett and Art Linkletter were chronicled in *TV Babylon;* to their ranks are added two other youthful victims.

Audra Lindley has had a long and successful TV career, costarring on *Bridget Loves Bernie* (1972) and, most notably, as Helen Roper on *Three's Company* (1977–1979) and *The Ropers* (1979). She had five children by two marriages—the second to actor James Whitmore—and for the last few years had devoted much of her time to helping her son John overcome his reliance on cocaine and alcohol.

"I tried to help John in every way," she said recently. "I sent him to so many places to try to cure him." She even went so far as to stay with him at these clinics, or nearby, so she could help him get through the programs.

Unfortunately, the unemployed airplane-plant worker could not be helped. Each time John got out of a treatment center, he fell back into the trap again. On February 22, 1990, the forty-five-year-old turned to drugs for the last time: he died of a drug overdose in his home in Gardena, California. Audra was in New Zealand at the time, and it was two days before anyone found him. A daughter phoned with the tragic news, and Audra hurried back.

"It was totally unexpected," Audra says through tears. "He had been through detox and had just gotten out." She reflects a moment, then says sadly, "I think that may be when you're more vulnerable."

There's some truth to that. After having had a support system, a patient comes out and has to face problems that haven't gone away, which drove them to drugs in the first place. Lamentably, even *with* a support system, many people find it just too tough to stay clean. Like John.

Tragic *and* surprising is the best way to describe the

story of another drug-addicted child, the daughter of America's favorite father.

Bill Cosby built his career around being as astute observer of human life—particularly as it pertains to children and families. Yet, he and his wife Camille have never been able to rein in the second of their five children, headstrong Erinn, who was born in 1966.

Since the age of nineteen, Erinn has abused drugs and alcohol. Her father says that the problem isn't substance abuse, per se, but is "behavioral. She's very stubborn. Since fourteen, Erinn has always said, 'I have to be me.' " Of all his children, Cosby says she is the only one "who is really very selfish."

After a brief stint at Spellman College in Atlanta, Erinn decided that academia was not for her. Moving to New York, she became a cocktail waitress—and a slave to a $200-a-day cocaine habit.

Erinn supported her habit for as long as she could, hopping from job to job, before finally writing to her parents and telling them about her addiction. The Cosbys resisted their initial impulse to run to her; that would only have caused a scene and accomplished nothing. Instead, they wrote back and pleaded with her to seek help.

In August of 1989, she did. She went to a drug treatment center in Newport, Rhode Island, and stayed for a month. After completing the program on September 24, she headed back to New York. Unable to find work, she sold an antique watch her parents had given to her on a birthday. It was worth $10,000; she got $3,000.

Reluctantly, Erinn decided to take a job at one of the clubs where she'd gone drinking and did drugs before her stay in the clinic. The pressure to slip back

Is *this* the real Bill Cosby . . . (© NBC-TV)

into old habits was great, and the money was in her pocket.

It was November. Two months was all it took for her to get back into drugs.

... or is *this*? Depends who you ask. (© Walt Disney Productions)

Her father was devastated when he learned of this. Aware that her habit would outstrip her earnings, he suspected that she might come home at some point in an effort to get money. Thus, Cosby took what he called the "tough love" route: he let her know that until she was clean, she wasn't welcomed at the house. As he painfully told *The Los Angeles Times*, "Right now we're estranged. She can't come here. She's not a person you can trust." He also said, "I've spent money, time, and had a lot of long talks with her trying to break through—but she's too far gone. As hard as it is for me to admit, there's nothing more I can do. She's on her own now."

Erinn's response was to flaunt her independence by marrying thirty-nine-year-old New York artist Edward Ruiz, whom she'd met in November at the nightclub Nell's. Their marriage, on January 17, 1990, took place in City Hall with a municipal judge performing the ten-minute ceremony; there were no family members present.

And yet, Erinn's impulsive act may yet be to her advantage. Reportedly, Ruiz has helped his wife stay away from drugs and limit her drinking to an occasional beer or glass of champagne.

Cosby will never stop hoping for a reconciliation. What's important, however, is that unlike Audra Lindley's son and so many others, Erinn is *alive*. Both Bill and Erinn Cosby are bright people and, in the fullness of time, with forgiveness on both sides, this tale may yet have a happy ending. Just like it would if it were on *The Cosby Show*.

A Dark Alley and Bad Grammer

Ted Danson of *Cheers* probably thought he had it bad when the press hinted (erroneously) that his marriage to wife Casey was in trouble and that he and former costar Shelley Long didn't get along all that well (not erroneously), or when a former housekeeper went public with the hair-raising news that the star wears a toupee. However, even Danson admits he's had it relatively easy compared with two of his costars.

"Kelsey Grammer's gotten a real bad rap," Danson said in an exclusive interview. "Has he made misjudgments? Who hasn't? Is he a junkie or a bad man? Uh-uh. No. He's a very *creative* man, and if he's got any demons—again, who hasn't?—he'll beat them."

Kelsey Grammer joined the cast of *Cheers* in 1984, the show's third season, playing smug, know-it-all psychiatrist Frasier Crane. The thirty-one-year-old, Virgin Islands-born actor and his wife Doreen had just had a daughter, Spencer, and life seemed good.

But then his marriage ended and, despite a healthy

income, Grammer moved into a surprisingly ramshackle home in Van Nuys. Tied to the front gate is a piece of torn cardboard with the address hand-lettered. Sharing the small, one-story house is Cerlette Lamme, a former professional ice skater who is four years his junior.

Grammer's first encounter with the law was in 1986, when he was given a ten-day jail sentence—later suspended—for reportedly failing to pay $52,000 in child support and alimony. He hadn't done that maliciously; it was a failure to organize himself and get it done. The not-so-gentle reminder served that purpose, and the event received little press—unlike Grammer's second run-in with the law.

In July of 1987, police stopped the actor on the suspicion that he was driving under the influence of alcohol. Checking Grammer's records, they found a slew of infractions. To begin with, there was an arrest warrant out on him for an unpaid speeding ticket. He was also driving without a license: actually, he'd never bothered to get anything more than a learner's permit. Again, none of this had been malice on Grammer's part, just absentminded neglect. Rather than go to jail for six months, he requested probation and permission to enter a rehabilitation program for the drinking. The request was granted. Unfortunately, Grammer never went.

The producers of *Cheers* were concerned about the incident. They knew that Grammer was a lusty drinker and were concerned not only because it might affect his work on the show, but because the last thing they wanted was to have an immoderate drinker appearing on a show set in a bar.

Grammer promised to be good. And he *was* sincere; he just couldn't quite pull it off.

In April of 1988, police noticed that Grammer was driving with expired tags. They pulled him over and escorted him to the patrol car while they ran a check on him. As Grammer was sitting there, a quarter of a gram of cocaine fell from his pocket. He was arrested and, in lieu of jailtime, was ordered to enter a drug rehabilitation program.

Once again, he didn't go. And on May 2, he failed to show up in court for a progress report. The date was rescheduled, and on May 19 Grammer told Judge Aviva K. Bobb that he'd been distracted because of personal problems: according to Grammer's attorney—former child star Robert Diamond of *Fury* fame—Cerlette was suffering bloody seizures due to "pressure on her sinuses, pushing on her nerves."

The judge was moved. He remarked, "We all have other responsibilities." He released Grammer on $7,500 bail, ordered him to attend rehabilitation, and rescheduled the hearing for October 25, 1989.

Strike three: Grammer failed to show. Exhibiting more generosity than they would have with an ordinary felon, the court gave the star another chance. He was told once again to enter a drug rehabilitation program—and, again, he didn't go. When he missed another court date in April, an arrest warrant was issued. But Grammer was nowhere to be found.

He had a reason, and it was more than forgetfulness this time. Cerlette had undergone surgery to correct her sinus problem and, when it was successful, Grammer was so happy he took her on a two-week cruise down the Mexican coast.

When the couple came back, the actor showed up

for his new court date. On May 16, he sat in the courtroom as *Cheers* costar Kirstie Alley came to testify on his behalf, talking about how difficult it had been for her to conquer her own drug problem. About how she'd dropped out of college, became an interior decorator, and "snorted up all my profits" before entering the drug rehabilitation program Narconon.

But while Municipal Court Commissioner Patricia Gorner Schwartz was impressed with Kirstie's recov-

A scruffy, dejected Kelsey Grammer listening in Van Nuys Municipal Court as he's ordered to stand trial on a felony drug charge. (AP/Wide Word)

ery, she felt it had no bearing on her costar, and she ordered Grammer to do one day of hard labor, picking up trash by the roadside, after which it was off to jail for failing to attend any of the rehabilitation classes.

Grammer dutifully put in the day of work, then showed up in Van Nuys Municipal Court. Carrying only a toothbrush, he was taken to jail and imprisoned alone in a Spartan ten-by-twelve-foot cell.

At a hearing in July, Grammer was informed that he would have to stand trial on the charge of possessing cocaine. The judge rejected attorney Diamond's request to give the actor another chance to complete a drug treatment program now that the problems with Cerlette were behind him.

Diamond said apologetically, "He's just easily distracted. He's a really talented guy. The only thing he isn't good at is appointments and dates. He was counting on his girlfriend; she normally would have reminded him (of the court dates). He leads a life where people continually tell him what to do the next day."

That's true; call sheets advise actors when to be ready the next day, and cars are dispatched to bring them to the studio. However, Deputy District Attorney Teri Hutchinson was disinclined to give Grammer another chance: she said, "He's not going to get a free ride."

Grammer was given three years probation—a charitable sentence, all things considered. And did it cause the actor to go straight? Not at all. In January of 1991, he was sentenced to an additional two years probation and ordered to undergo drug testing after he admitted using cocaine while the show was taping an episode in Boston.

The question is, when all of this is over, will Grammer learn his lesson? That's difficult to say. The pressures to fall back into bad habits are especially great in TV, where a performer can be the nova-hot costar of the top-rated show one day and glacially cold the next. Those kinds of ups and downs don't encourage stability. On the other hand, Grammer has been hit hard enough and often enough and publicly enough to *want* to get clean. More important, viewers like him and his future could be bright—provided he gets clean and stays that way. In the end, that may be reason enough for him to succeed.

Even though Grammer's problems made the newspapers every step of the way—adding embarrassment but little impetus to reform—he's still just a costar on *Cheers*. Not only is Kirstie Alley a bigger name who had previously starred in the spy series *Masquerade* (1983) and the miniseries *North and South* (1985), she also starred in a hit film, *Look Who's Talking* (1989). That makes her a bigger target. And in 1984 she married relatively well-known TV actor, Parker Stevenson, of *The Hardy Boys Mysteries* (1977–1979), *Falcon Crest* (1984), and *Baywatch* (1989), which makes them both bigger targets still.

Ironically, Kirstie's biggest problem, cocaine addiction, was something she'd beat years before becoming a star. She began using the stuff in 1979, when she was twenty-four. She was working as an interior decorator and had a habit that cost her $400 a week. "I was whacked out of my mind for two years," she says. "I was a drug addict and was very irresponsible."

After her mother was killed by a drunk driver in 1981, Kirstie took stock of her addiction: entering a drug rehabilitation program, she kicked the habit and has been clean ever since. Early in 1989, she even gave up cigarettes and, today, Kirstie lectures widely in schools about the dangers of cocaine. She's let it be known that her home is open to kids in trouble.

But appearing at Grammer's trial and revealing her drug addiction is not the only reason Kirstie made news.

First, there were rumors of a rift in the marriage. Kirstie was seen at screenings and other public functions with *Cheers* costar Woody Harrelson, which started tongues wagging, while the tabloids suggested that a romance with Ted Danson was destroying *both* of their marriages.

Kirstie adamantly denied that she was romantically involved with either man, telling one reporter, "When some people see a happily married couple, they get jealous and resentful. They don't have that kind of contentment or commitment in their lives, so they don't want anyone else to, either." She confided, "But I'm getting fed up with [the rumors]. Why don't they just leave us alone?"

Because she was a big, beautiful target whose name sold papers. And while Kirstie was busy defending herself against those allegations in 1989 and into 1990, a strangely contradictory charge surfaced.

It was a small line in *The Village Voice*, and it appeared in the column of gay writer Michael Musto in June of 1990. It read, "That cheery TV actress is a daughter of Sappho and her husband is a hardy, and gay, boy." The allusions weren't exactly subtle, and though, in an interview, Musto wouldn't confirm that he was referring to the stars of *Cheers* and *The Hardy Boys Mysteries*, he did say, "I have great sources."

Parker's publicist, Jim Dobson, says, "Kirstie and

Parker both say it's just too stupid to comment on."
Later, Kirstie herself said, "It's funny in a pathetic
way. It must be a last resort to find something controversial about us." But whether or not there's any truth
to the inference, the seed has been planted. Regardless of how many denials are issued, people will always
have their doubts. Whether that affects the credibility
of Kirstie or Parker as romantic leads remains to be
seen.

The irony of being called both heterosexually un-
faithful and gay hasn't been lost on Kirstie, but it does
make her wonder what kind of mad business she's
in—and whether or not things can possibly get worse.

Knowing TV Babylon, it most certainly can.

An Unpleasant "Outing"

It's a relatively new use of the press (or misuse, depending upon your point of view): it's called "outing," and it's the publishing of articles identifying gay celebrities by name in an effort to force them to come out of the closet and publicly acknowledge their homosexuality.

"Each coming out by famous people equals three years of hard work by activists toward a world where gays and lesbians are no longer hated and discriminated against," says Rex Wochner of the gay Chicago newspaper *Outline*. "Revealing Rock Hudson was gay equaled five years of activism." Defending "outing," Wochner says that there are three reasons for doing it. First, it's news. Second, there's nothing wrong with being gay. And third, he maintains, "At a certain level of hypocrisy, invasion of privacy becomes the lesser of two evils."

Gunther Freehill, of the gay activist group ACT UP, adds, "It's important that people know that in

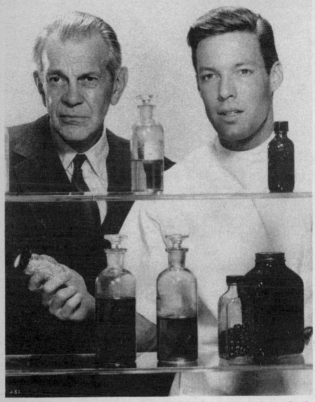

Richard Chamberlain as *Dr. Kildare* in 1961, a heartthrob to millions of young girls. (Howard Frank Collection)

society lots of people are gay and lesbian. There are going to be short-term costs, but in the long run it will be best."

The highest-profile victim of the "short-term costs" has been Richard Chamberlain. Born in 1935, the actor has starred in the classic series *Dr. Kildare* (1961–1966) and the flop *Island Son* (1989), in highly rated miniseries such as *Centennial* (1978), *Shogun* (1980), and *The Thorn Birds* (1983), as well as several made-for-TV movies including the highly praised *Wallenberg: A Hero's Story* (1985) and, ironically, *The Woman I Love* (1972) and *Casanova* (1987).

There had been rumors about Chamberlain's homosexuality for years. Reportedly, when he was working on the theatrical film *Joy in the Morning* in 1965, a homophobic female costar learned he was gay and viciously taunted him while spreading the word. Pat Burke, editor of the gay publication *Update*, says, "It's been around in Hollywood that Chamberlain has been gay for more than twenty-five years. But he was never part of the pack with Sal Mineo and that whole crowd."

The news went from being local gossip to hitting the mainstream press in January 1990, when the French magazine *Nous Deux* published an interview with the actor, in which he's said to have claimed, "I've had enough pretending, and it's too bad for people who are upset by it." The article named former ballet dancer Martin Rabbett as his gay lover of many years, told about Chamberlain's huge donations to AIDS research after the AIDS-related death of a close friend, John Allison, and contained other revelations. Even though the author was anonymous, the editors adamantly believed in the veracity of the interview. It came to the attention of the U.S. media when it was reprinted in *Update*.

Through his publicist, Annett Wolf, Chamberlain said he'd never given an interview to anyone from *Nous Deux*, and adamantly denied being gay. "Rich-

Chamberlain today, his appeal intact. (UPI/Bettmann)

ard is appalled this is being reported in the gay newspapers," Annett said. "Richard is shocked that everyone's running this. Richard is not gay. It's simply not true." Chamberlain himself says that he's never married because, "I have sort of been married to my career."

What about Mr. Rabbett, whom Chamberlain met during the making of *The Thorn Birds*, and who was credited as co-executive producer and co-creator of *Island Son*? Chamberlain *does* live with him in a mountaintop mansion in Hawaii but, fearful of being photographed together (even an innocent picture of the two could have been interpreted and captioned in any number of provocative ways), they always drove to the *Island Son* set separately, and sat well away from each other while they were there.

Chamberlain's associates insist that Martin is the actor's assistant, nothing more, and Chamberlain describes the attempted "outing" as the fabrications of "homosexual terrorists." But Harold Fairbanks, a reporter who covers the Hollywood scene for gay magazines, claims to know several men who have slept with Chamberlain.

Regardless, the matter doesn't appear to have hurt the actor's marketability. Either his fans don't believe it (Liberace's didn't, either, it should be noted), don't care (which is how it should be), or feel sorry for the way his personal life has been dragged before the public eye. In fact, the "outing" attempt may actually have backfired by making the gay activists look like prying bad guys.

If the truth be told, most publications, straight and gay alike, have shown remarkable restraint where gay Hollywood is concerned. For example, actor George

George Maharis between takes on *Route 66*, seen here with guest star Julie Newmar. (Howard Frank Collection)

Maharis of *Route 66* (1960–1963), has never pretended to be other than what he is. He frequented gay bars regularly in his youth, was once arrested at a gas station for lewd behavior, and lived with a gay roommate, Danny Collins, from 1976 until 1990, when Collins died from complications of AIDS (Maharis tested negatively for the disease). Perhaps because he is a relatively minor star, the press let him be. Paul Lynde died before "outing" was in vogue, but two macho TV action stars—both married for the sake of image—have had gay experiences that could easily have been exposed. Similarly, a former TV comedienne, now a screen and stage star, who has been living with her gay lover for years. And a former talk-show host . . . and the head of an extended TV family . . . the list goes on.

Though the "outing" of stars will certainly become more pronounced as the frustration of activists grows, the majority of the "bedroom tales" these days are coming from former lovers of the stars, who can be persuaded to talk to magazines or tabloids for from $10,000 to $100,000 per story.

Kristy McNichol, star of the hit series *Empty Nest*, had appeared in TV commercials since 1968, when she was six years old. Her first series was the short-lived *Apple's Way* (1974), after which she gained fame—and a pair of Emmy awards—for her portrayal as Letitia "Buddy" Lawrence on the series *Family* (1976–1980).

From 1983 to 1985, Kristy reportedly had an ongoing love affair with female model Melisande Casey, who has since talked in considerable detail about the relationship. Melisande says that Kristy had her first intimate encounter with a woman at the age of twelve, when she was fondled by a baby-sitter. The incident proved to be a catalyst. Kristy's regard for men had always been low; her mother, Carollyne, had been divorced when Kristy was three and, according to Melisande, Kristy "had been turned off men by seeing her mother going through one romance after another."

Kristy's lesbian lifestyle was not an especially well-kept secret. Melisande says that during the period when she was dating Kristy, two gay men lived at the house with them in the Hollywood Hills, ready to be

Kristy McNichol visits brother Jimmy on the set of the movie *Thrilled to Death*. Jimmy's "hatchet job" wasn't nearly as grim as the one done by the press. (UPI/Bettman)

seen with Kristy at a moment's notice. Kristy also went to lesbian parties and bars, and Harold Fairbanks says, "I've seen Kristy McNichol shopping at gay stores for years—others have too—and she was left alone."

In the spring of 1990, Melisande went public with details about their love life, describing Kristy's fantasies of Bo Derek, and telling how, the first time they made love, "She started growling and barking like a dog. She then began biting me like a pooch." There were also tales about how they went dancing with drag queens, stimulated each other with Emotion Lotion, and more. They finally broke up because Melisande wanted to see men as well, and "Kristy was too jealous. It was either all or nothing."

Kristy herself denies the allegations, calling them "complete lies." She insists that she hopes to marry one day and raise children, and says that the reason she hasn't sued over the stories about her private life is, "I don't have the time or patience (and) that only generates more negative press."

In any case, the sensational stories haven't seemed to hurt her or the ratings of her popular series. Again, either viewers don't believe the stories, don't care, or feel sorry that her private life has been made so public.

The sex life of former *Welcome Back, Kotter* star John Travolta has also been discussed in vivid detail by a former male lover, a forty-one-year-old porn star Paul Barresi. Travolta's representatives deny the stories, but Barresi has photos of himself and Travolta together. The bodybuilder first met Travolta in 1982. Barresi was working out at a Los Angeles gym and went outside to see a friend off when he was spotted by John, who was having lunch across the street. Much to Barresi's surprise, when he went back in and stepped into the shower, Travolta walked over. The actor said he was a "big fan" of Barresi's, and asked him to dinner. Though Barresi says that he himself is straight, "Some men in Hollywood . . . find me attractive, and . . . I've let them use me in the hopes of furthering my acting career.'' That night, after giving each other massages, Barresi says the two became lovers.

During the next two years, Travolta reportedly paid Barresi $400 each time they were together, not only sleeping with him but talking about Travolta's bisexu-

John Travolta with Olivia Newton-John. (© Twentieth Century-Fox)

ality and various female lovers—and his crush on Burt Reynolds. "I love to watch Burt Reynolds movies and fantasize," Travolta allegedly told Barresi. For his part, Travolta got Barresi a small part in his film *Perfect*.

After two years, Barresi married and the relationship cooled, although Barresi says he and Travolta still talk on the phone from time to time, and have had lunch on a few occasions. Presumably, Travolta—who became engaged to actress Kelly Preston on New Year's Eve, 1990—won't be picking up the tab now that Barresi's gone the tell-all route.

Once in a rare while, however, an alleged ex-lover's efforts to spill the beans about a TV star backfire, as in the case of Andre Pavon.

In 1970, at the age of nineteen, Pavon appeared in the Broadway show *Purlie* with then-thirty-two-year-old Sherman Hemsley. When they met, they became good friends who made a deal: if either of them ever made it big, they would help the other out. When Hemsley struck gold on *The Jeffersons*, he says, "I kept my end of the bargain. In 1975 I gave Andre a room in my Hollywood Hills home and helped him out financially."

That much, they both agree on. However, Pavon says they were more than friends: he says they were lovers. They parted after several years, and when Hemsley next heard from his friend it was in May of 1990, when Pavon phoned and asked the *Amen* star for $30,000. If the money wasn't forthcoming, Pavon said he was going to peddle his story to the highest bidder.

Hemsley didn't pay, and Pavon went straight to the tabloids, offering them lurid details of the relationship for $30,000. No one took the bait. Instead (for free), they published Hemsley's version of events.

According to the actor, in the early 1980s, Pavon started using drugs. Hemsley says he tried to help him, but "When it became clear I couldn't stop his slide into addiction, I made the painful decision to kick him out, hoping it would shock him into straightening out his life." That didn't work, and in 1985 Pavon was arrested twice on drug charges. He went to jail and, a month before he was to be released, phoned Hemsley with his extortionary demand for the money.

Any damage Pavon might have done to the star's reputation was minimized because Hemsley went to the press; by presenting his side first, Hemsley rendered Pavon's charges anticlimactic.

On the opposite end of the spectrum, there have occasionally been celebrities who come out of the closet willingly. When they do so, it's usually because they are proud of who they are—such as Terry Sweeney, a *Saturday Night Live* regular (1985–1986 season)—or because they need the publicity. Former *Rowan and Martin's Laugh-In* star Judy Carne, the "sock-it-to-me" lady, had faded into obscurity when she went public with details of her sex life and catastrophoic marriage to Burt Reynolds, which lasted from 1963 to 1966.

Talking to the gay publications *The Advocate* and *OutWeek*, among others, Judy said that it was while she was married to Burt and living in Hollywood that she discovered the joys of woman-to-woman love.

At the time there was a lot of tension in the marriage, because while Burt could only land a supporting role in *Gunsmoke*—he played blacksmith Quint Asper, from 1962 to 1965—she was starring in a succession of series: *Fair Exchange* (1962), *The Baileys of Balboa* (1964), and *Love on a Rooftop* (1966). She says that her husband's ego "couldn't take that (and) Burt beat me up."

One night, after Burt "threw me against our fireplace and cracked my skull," Judy went out to a bar where she met "one of the most beautiful women I'd ever seen . . . the daughter of one of the most famous screen actors of all time."

The woman was a lesbian, and though Judy says she had never thought of a woman in a sexual way before, she felt "so brutalized and so violated" that she "couldn't bear to be touched by a man." Judy went to the woman's house, where they made "delicious" love and, eventually, Judy moved in with her. She adds that in addition to everything else, Burt had an extremely difficult time handling the fact "that from him, I turned to another woman."

Judy and the woman ended up living together for almost two years, during which time Judy says her lover "put me back together emotionally." After they parted, Judy had affairs with other women, including a well-known singer.

Her stint on *Laugh-In* lasted from 1968 to 1970, after which she guest-starred on several episodes of *Love, American Style.* Among her colleagues, Judy made no secret of her sexual preferences, and that cost her many parts: if the public knew that she was sleeping with women, any of the light, romantic shows on which she might guest star would suffer. (She recalls one producer shouting at her, "You dyke! Are you crazy? Career suicide?") Her only TV job during this period came in 1975, in an episode of the police

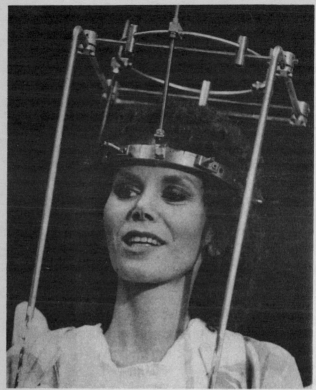

Judy Carne in 1978, suffering from a fractured vertebra. Is it the result of having it socked to her once too often? No— she'd been in a car accident in New Hope, Pennsylvania. Sadly, that would prove to be the least of her ills. (UPI/ Bettmann)

series *Get Christie Love*, which featured many of the *Laugh-In* stars.

Because of deep depression, she says, "I tried to destroy myself" with drugs. The latter half of the 1970s and much of the 1980s were, for Judy, a constant battle with narcotics and abstinence, with the latter rarely triumphant. Although she was acquitted on charges of heroin possession in the United States in 1978, she was fined $720 in an English court in 1982 for possessing a small amount of cocaine. There were other brushes with the law, but by her fiftieth birthday

Carne goes to court in Uxbridge, England, in 1985, to face drug smuggling charges. (AP/Wide World)

in 1989, Judy had come to grips with the problem and cleaned herself up. Sexually, she seemed to try to pull back slightly by stating that she considered herself bisexual: "I see an attractive man, I see an attractive woman, it really doesn't matter," she said.

Ironically, drug free and trying to get work again, she came to the United States from England and was immediately arrested: there was an outstanding warrant from Hamilton County, Ohio, issued in 1979, seeking Carne on charges of drug abuse. After her arrest at John F. Kennedy International Airport in New York, the actress was taken to Queens to be booked. The charges were eventually dropped, and Judy is trying to rebuild her life with the help of her good friend and hairdresser, twenty-four-year-old Mike Gregg. It's fair to say, however, that the only place for Judy on TV will be doing a *Geraldo* or *Donahue* where her troubled life, and not her talents as an actress, will be on display.

Strokes of Bad Luck

If ever a show can be described as cursed, *Diff'rent Strokes* is definitely it.

The series debuted on NBC on Friday, November 3, 1978, and ran until 1986. The half-hour sitcom was about two black brothers—eight-year-old Arnold and twelve-year-old Willis—whose mother, a housekeeper, dies and leaves them to her white employer, wealthy Philip Drummond. Drummond is delighted to add the boys to his Park Avenue household, which includes his daughter Kimberly. Though characters came and went over the years (including a wife for Philip, Maggie, played by Dixie Carter), these four formed the hub of the show.

Young, cherubic Gary Coleman starred as Arnold, Todd Bridges was Willis, Conrad Bain played Philip, and Dana Plato was Kimberly. Bain came through the series unscathed; it was the kids who suffered.

Coleman was actually something of a marvel. Born in 1968, he was not only a natural actor with enormous appeal, but he was a survivor. Because he was born with his right kidney atrophied and his left kidney in danger of failing, he underwent a transplant when he was six, a procedure that stunted his growth and limited his activities. He became a model because it was something he could do without fear of hurting himself.

After several years of starring in commercials, Coleman was spotted by producer Norman Lear, who developed *Diff'rent Strokes* for him. Gary and the show were a hit. Even when his new kidney began to fail in 1982, forcing to go on a portable dialysis machine until a second transplant in 1984, the youngster's spirits and enthusiasm remained undimmed.

Todd Bridges was three years older than Gary, even though he, too, had begun acting when he was six. Prior to *Diff'rent Strokes*, he'd been featured in the series *Fish* as cute little Loomis. Dana Plato, the oldest of the three children, was born in 1964. This was the native Californian's first series.

When the series ended, each of the kids faced heartbreak and disappointment in ways as divergent as they were devastating.

Plato, the divorced mother of a four-year-old son, Tyler, found herself typecast after *Diff'rent Strokes* went off the air. "I've lost a lot of roles because people still see me as the girl next door," she complained in April of 1989. Worse, though she'd been earning $22,000 an episode on the show, she discovered that an adviser had not only run off with all her money, but had never paid the taxes on it. Dana wasn't just broke, she owed the IRS $128,000. Her residual earnings from the series were attached, and Tyler went to live with her husband Lanny because Dana couldn't support him.

Desperate to do something attention getting, she accepted an offer from *Playboy* magazine to pose nude. Unfortunately, the June pictorial did not bring her adult roles, as she'd hoped—just a single offer, she says, "for a triple X-rated hardcore adult film."

Dana's mother had died of cancer in January of 1988 and, with nowhere to go, she moved in with her grandmother in Las Vegas. But, says Dana, "My grandmother told me she didn't want me around! She said I had too much energy and that I got on her nerves." Dana moved out and got a succession of jobs: as a receptionist, as a salesperson in an art gallery and, most recently, at a dry cleaner's, working for $5.75 an hour.

Living in a small apartment with her boyfriend, a warehouse worker, Plato spent time and money in the Lakes Lounge down the street, playing the slot machines. On February 28, with her rent due and not enough money to pay it, she applied for a second job, picking up trash and cleaning bathrooms in her building. Dana didn't get it and in desperation, she donned a black hat, coat, and sunglasses and went to a nearby video store. Reportedly drawing a pellet gun from her coat pocket, she told the clerk to give her all the money in the cash register. The employee handed her $164. After Plato left, the clerk called the police and calmly reported, "I've just been robbed by the girl who played Kimberly on *Diff'rent Strokes*."

Plato was arrested and taken to the Clark County Detention Center. She was held for five days and allowed to leave only after singer Wayne Newton generously posted the $13,00 bail.

Plato has pleaded innocent to the crime. There are those who claim that she not only did it, she did it for the publicity. The still attractive twenty-six-year-old has not given up her dream of making a comeback in TV but, as the Vegas resident knows, the cards are stacked against her.

Still, people have come back from deeper down in the hole—witness one of Plato's costars, Todd Bridges.

His first bout with the law occurred when Bridges was sixteen years old and the show was still on the air. Bridges was arrested, cuffed, and pushed to the ground in his driveway after getting out of his car: police mistook his $30,000 Porsche for one that had been stolen recently in the same neighborhood.

Though Bridges cried racism, it was an honest mistake. Moreover, he was reportedly indignant when they first approached, fueling their suspicions.

Shortly thereafter, Bridges got a ticket for riding a motorbike on the sidewalk. A white friend who had been riding alongside him was not cited. Once again, though, Bridges is said to have baited the police after the initial warning to get off the sidewalk, prompting their action.

A series of tickets and a six-month suspension of his license followed, after which things really went downhill for the teenager. In 1983, when police in Beverly Hills stopped Bridges for speeding, they looked in his car and found a loaded .45 semiautomatic. Bridges said that he needed it for protection: he claimed that the KKK had shot at him and that he'd been subjected to racial slurs. The authorities didn't buy the story, and Bridges was fined $240 and placed on twelve months' probation for carrying the gun.

Bridges was earning $40,000 an episode when

Diff'rent Strokes was canceled. Because the young man was so closely identified with the role of Willis, he found it impossible to get work: for solace, he stupidly turned to cocaine.

"I had to sell everything," Bridges would later explain. "I couldn't quit [the habit]. I couldn't say no."

His perceptions distorted by drugs, each new run-in with the law seemed to make the teenager more belligerent, and not just with the police. In March of 1986, he took his car to a garage to have it customized. He told owner Greg Tyree that if the work weren't completed on time, he was going to shoot Tyree and blow up every car on the property. Naturally, Tyree didn't take the cocky kid seriously.

Bridges returned prematurely, on March 25, and was furious when the work wasn't done. The next day, Tyree's 1971 Mercedes was blown sky-high.

Police searched Bridges' house in the San Fernando Valley, where they found guns and plastic bags containing what looked like gunpowder. Bridges plea-bargained his way out of serious jail time: charges for the actual bombing, for possession of a bomb, and for possession of materials to make a bomb were all dropped in exchange for a plea of no contest on the threat to bomb the car. He didn't go to jail for that, but would have been better off if he had: the worst was yet to come.

The twenty-three-year-old Bridges took to hanging out at a crack house in south central Los Angeles, where twenty-five-year-old Kenneth Clay also spent a lot of time. A security man there, Clay had been convicted of drug dealing in Texas and had come to L.A. in violation of his probation.

Todd Bridges heads for arraignment on misdemeanor weapons charges in 1983. No one knew it then, but Bridges was already on a pathetic downward spiral, which would result in many more court appearances. (UPI/Bettmann)

For a while, Bridges had money. He had money from the show, and had won an out-of-court settlement stemming from a 1987 lawsuit in which he accused his former accountant of embezzling $400,000. But that ran out fast, and, desperate for drug money, Bridges is said to have begun stealing things from the crack house—mostly guns—and selling them.

On February 2, 1989, Clay confronted Bridges about the thefts, and they argued over that and other matters, including Clay's alleged theft of the actor's BMW. Bridges stormed off, only to return later with a friend, Harvie Eugene Duckett, and a .22 caliber gun.

As Clay would later describe it, Bridges was " 'based out" and in "the worst" shape he'd ever seen him. "He looked like his eyes were about to jump out of his head. He'd lost a lot of weight, just wasn't himself." That was an understatement: as Bridges himself later revealed, "I used cocaine around the clock for four days."

While Duckett growled, "Shoot him, shoot him," Bridges reportedly pistol-whipped Clay, then stood back and, shouting, "I told you Tex! I told you Tex!" pumped six bullets into him, stopping only when he heard the hammer clicking. He's said to have run off then; miraculously, Clay survived. Bridges was arrested and charged with first-degree attempted murder. Municipal Court Judge David Horowitz set bail at $2 million.

Since Bridges could not post bail, he was locked up in Los Angeles County Jail—not the ideal place for the scared, drugless, and friendless kid. Two weeks later, on February 22, he went berserk. Throwing himself against the side of his cell and wailing repeatedly, "I'm going to end it all!" Bridges took off his shirt, tied one end to a crossbar of the cell door, knotted the other end around his neck, and sagged toward the floor in an attempt to choke himself. Guards reached him before he could succeed, and Bridges was taken to a padded cell in the psychiatric wing.

Bridges seemed to recover his composure in the days that followed, and was returned to his cell.

Mistake.

Stealing a spoon from his dinner tray, the young man sharpened an edge by rubbing it against the cell floor and, on February 24, screaming that he was going to end his life, Bridges punctured his wrist. Guards entered his cell and Bridges struggled violently to prevent them from subduing him. It took four men to pin him so that the prison doctor could stitch the wound. Bridges was once again placed in a padded cell where he was lashed to a bed and placed under constant observation.

Psychiatric evaluation determined that neither of the suicide attempts was sincere, and on February 28 he was returned to his cell where, for days, he did nothing but cry.

Bridges spent a total of nine months in jail before the case went to trial. There, in exchange for testimony, Duckett agreed to plead no contest to being an accessary after the fact, and was put on three years' probation. As for Bridges, he told the court that he had a serious cocaine habit and was in dreadful financial shape. He cried repeatedly on the stand, insisting that he didn't even remember shooting Clay. "That's one of the side effects of the drugs," he said.

Apparently, the jury felt that Bridges was sufficiently sincere and repentant, and acquitted him on the charge of attempted involuntary manslaughter. But they couldn't decide on the matter of assault with a deadly weapon, and that charge was refiled. In the meantime, he was set free.

And what did the young man do with his free time? Clean up his act? No way.

Just a few months later, on May 5, police noticed
a car parked outside a Van Nuys bookstore at 3:50
in the morning. The two occupants obviously weren't
waiting for it to open, so the officers approached the
car. Bridges and a friend, Steve Mallen, were told to
get out: upon searching the car, police found 48 grams
of cocaine. Bridges was held on $25,000 bail, but was
released because, as Deputy District Attorney Norm
Shapiro said, "After evaluation, it's rather clear there
is insufficient evidence to show he had any control of
the substance."

Right. It was in the car by chance.

In August of 1990, Bridges was tried for assault.
Prosecutors contended that Bridges admitted to the
attack when police arrested him. Defense attorney
Johnnie Cochran countered that Bridges was so coked
up he couldn't have done it. Cochran maintained that
Duckett had done the shooting; the jury believed him.
As for Duckett, he'd pleaded guilty to an accessory
charge and had been granted leniency for cooperating
with the prosecution.

After the last drug arrest, Bridges' mother Betty
said sadly, "Todd has destroyed his life with drugs,
and I feel that the arrest is God's way of trying to
help him." However, Todd was also trying to help
himself. Sobered by the events of the past few years
he decided to go back to work and, immediately after
the trial, got a part on the syndicated series *The New
Lassie*. The role? Bridges starred as a deputy sheriff.
According to a publicist on the set, Bridges, "Looked
good. Todd is clean." He also married Rebecca San
Filipo on November 14, 1989, with whom he'd been
living since 1985, and has begun working on a book
about his tribulations and trials. Unfortunately, while

the book is well on track, the marriage was short-lived, Rebecca filing for divorce in December of 1990, citing—what else?—irreconcilable differences.

In contrast to his two costars, Gary Coleman's life wasn't ruined by *Diff'rent Strokes:* in fact, financially he's rather well off. His fortune is estimated at more than $7 million, he earns approximately $750,000 a year, and he's continued to work, making TV movies and starring in series such as *227* in which—talk about breaking a stereotype!—he played a thug.

But despite the fame and employment, all has not been well in the young actor's life. Not by a long shot.

Healthwise, the twenty-one-year-old, four-foot, eight-inch-tall actor has had ongoing problems, most notably three kidney transplants since 1986. But the greatest heartbreak stems from a rift with the parents who had nurtured Coleman's career.

The problems began when the elder Colemans, William and Edmonia Sue, sat their seventeen-year-old son down in the Cheviot Hills, California, home they all shared, and informed him that he was adopted. They said that they hadn't told him before because he had enough to worry about with his health and career.

Gary didn't take the news well. In a book the family had written in 1981, *Gary Coleman, Medical Miracle,* Mrs. Coleman had penned a poignant account of her son's birth. If *that* wasn't true, Gary reasoned, what else in their lives had been a lie? Did they even love him?

His parents said that of *course* their love for him was sincere, but the angry Gary moved out of the house and, shortly thereafter, had a thundering fight with his father. The fight spilled outdoors, Gary ending it when he climbed into a car and reportedly tried to run William down.

Tensions increased over the next few months, to the point where Gary fired his parents as his personal managers and trustees, and also got rid of his attorneys, publicist, and agent. But from the point of view of his parents and former advisers, Gary's most con-

Gary Coleman triumphant. The actor leaves a Los Angeles courtroom in 1990 after successfully fighting his mother's efforts to take charge of his financial affairs. (AP/Wide World)

troversial move was naming a friend, Dion Mial, to manage his career and finances. Mial, twenty-three, was an unemployed Michael Jackson impersonator whom Gary had hired for $325 a week to be his driver and assistant. The move convinced Gary's parents that Mial had somehow "brainwashed" their son—either that, or Gary's kidney problems were causing psychological traumas in addition to "short-term or long-term memory loss."

As the actor's former agent Vic Perillo put it, "The last time I saw Gary, his face had a grayish cast. He was also speaking in an incoherent, repetitive fashion," suggesting to Perillo that he was skipping dialysis treatments.

If Gary's parents weren't startled enough, they were in for a real shock in February of 1989, when he filed a legal action against them and his former business manager to get an accounting of his financial affairs. Gary said at the time, it was "an agonizing decision [but] the only alternative I had in trying to take charge of my own career and personal affairs as an adult."

The suit hurt his parents deeply and, after pondering the situation, Mrs. Coleman reluctantly filed a petition of her own in December of 1989, seeking to name the U.S. Trust Company of California to look after her son's "person and estate." Through her lawyer, she insisted that her interest was solely in Gary's well-being, and added that she and her husband had done nothing improper with Gary's finances—that, in fact, during the run of *Diff'rent Strokes*, they'd taken only 20 percent of his earnings when California law would have permitted them to claim nearly four times that amount.

Gary issued a stinging rebuttal, which said in part

that his mother's "legal action obviously stems from
her frustration at not being able to control my life."
Adding that he "was very hurt by the vindictive
response," he filed another suit in February of 1990,
charging malicious prosecution and claiming that his
parents' petition had "tarnished" his reputation in the
industry. He sought damages of $25,000, the amount
it cost him to fight the conservatorship maneuver.

When the charges and countercharges finished fly-
ing, the fight went to Gary: guided by a report from
independent counsel Arne S. Lindgren, who had been
appointed to interview Coleman, Los Angeles Superior Court Judge Martha Goldin found no cause for
Gary's affairs to be handed over to a conservator.
Gary turned around and sued his parents for another
$25,000 in damages for having put him through the
wringer "knowing that the allegations were false." Privately, he suspected that they'd gone to court because
bad investments and money spent on cars, houses, and
other big-ticket items had left them in troubled financial straits.

Coleman and Mial lived together for a while, divid-
ing their time between in homes in Los Angeles and
Denver, where Gary had a weekly radio program.
Then, after a few months, Gary suddenly and inexpli-
cably changed his lifestyle—drastically. He moved to
Tucson, Arizona, shaved his head, chunked-out,
changed his name to Andy Shane, invited a young
nineteen-year-old-woman, a local grocery clerk, to
move in with him, and spends his days playing video
games, watching movies, and driving around in the
desert. There have also been kidney problems that put
him in the hospital in 1990, but as of this writing Coleman has struggled back to health. Overall, his is a

lifestyle many young men would embrace if they had the means—but it's sad that yet another child star has ended up in self-imposed exile from the industry and his family.

Child Abuse

While there's fault on both sides in the Gary Coleman affair, some stories seem to have no gray in them whatsoever. Case in point: Danny Bonaduce, former costar of *The Partridge Family*, which aired from 1970 to 1974. Among the principal child cast members, Susan Dey (Laurie Partridge) made a few films and eventually got a juicy part on the hit series *L.A. Law*, while David Cassidy (Keith Partridge) had a separate recording career and has stuck with music, becoming a remarkably mature musician—despite his recent lament that "Beaver Cleaver was a deeper human being than people give *me* credit for."

But Danny Bonaduce, younger than the others, didn't have the maturity to deal with the end of the Partridge gravy train.

Ironically, it wasn't a lack of work that did it. Fifteen years old when the series ended, Danny went on to appear in TV movies and in episodes of various TV series, such as *CHiPS* and *California Fever*. He also did voices for cartoon series such as *Partridge Family: 2200 A.D.* and *Goober and the Ghost Chasers*. What did Danny in were drugs.

"I was a real confused kid," he says. "A lot of people think you do a television show, you immediately start taking drugs." He paused. "I did that."

The drug of choice was cocaine, and it helped to deprive Bonaduce of the $350,000 he'd saved while he was working. His decline culminated in an arrest in Hollywood for possession of cocaine in 1985. The charge was dropped after he attended a series of drug-counseling sessions.

Taking stock of his life, Bonaduce wisely abandoned TV for a career as a disc jockey. He got a job in Philadelphia, at WEGX-FM, aka Eagle 106, working the 10:00 P.M. to 2:00 A.M. stretch. His show was a smash, and he was earning $75,000 a year.

Outwardly, the chunky, cigarette-smoking Bonaduce seemed to have settled down. But he'd gone back to using drugs, even though he knew that they "never, ever did anything good for me."

Cut to March, 1990. While in Florida to appear on the USA Cable network show *Youthquake*, Bonaduce was arrested while buying crack in a Daytona Beach housing project. He spent twelve hours in jail before posting the $5,000 bond. WEGX general manager David Noll reluctantly took Bonaduce "off the air until we find out all the details."

When Bonaduce learned of his suspension, he says, "I was totally suicidal. I was having heart attacks about being fired. I knew if I lost my job I'd be screwed: no one else would touch me." And then there was guilt: "I couldn't believe I hurt the Eagle.

Even Carl Sagan can't figure out how stupid I am. I can barely look at myself."

Rather generously, the station said that Bonaduce would be permitted to return, provided he submit to company-paid drug counseling and weekly drug testing. Bonaduce was happy to agree, and spent thirty-one days at a rehabilitation center in Reading, PA. "It was a nice experience," he said upon his return. More important, after making "a monumental fool" of himself, Bonaduce said that the bust forced him to take serious stock of his life. "Thinking about where I could have been [if he hadn't taken drugs] gives me the shivers. I really think that drugs are badly weakening the fiber of America."

After cleaning himself up, Bonaduce decided that he needed a change of scenery and moved to Phoenix, where he became a DJ at KKFR radio. Unfortunately, his problems didn't end with the move. Early on March 31, 1991, Bonaduce reportedly picked up a twenty-four-year-old transvestite prostitute, Darius Lee Barney, and offered him twenty dollars for sex. When Barney refused, Bonaduce is said to have beat him. Police were alerted after area residents heard Barney's screams; when officers approached the car, it sped off. The police gave chase, pursuing Bonaduce by car and helicopter through downtown Phoenix at speeds of up to ninety miles an hour. He was finally stopped and arrested. Released on his own recognizance, the DJ disputes the police report—even though there was blood on his hands, boots, and car when he was arrested.

While drugs gave Bonaduce his push down the slopes of ruin, alcohol hasn't been doing a hell of a lot of good for the country either. No one typifies that more than the former costar of *Eight is Enough*, twenty-two year-old Adam Rich. Rich, who played the moppet Nicholas on the series that aired from 1977 to 1981, became hooked on alcohol and cocaine as a teenager. After years of abuse, he checked into the Betty Ford Center in May of 1988. His manager, Jeff Ballard, said at the time that Rich was "determined to straighten out his life."

Unfortunately, good intentions alone don't do it. On October 6, 1990, sheriff's deputies stopped Rich at 1:00 A.M. as he was driving through West Hollywood. He made an illegal U-turn and stopped at a crosswalk when there wasn't a pedestrian in sight. As soon as one approached, Rich drove across.

Tests revealed that Rich's blood alcohol level was .18 percent—more than double the legal level. The young actor spent the night in jail, and later told the press, "Look, I'm ashamed about what happened. What people don't realize is that a setback like this is all part of the recovery process. It's all a part of getting better, which I'm going to do." Judge Judith Stein wasn't terribly moved by his disclaimers, and sentenced him to five years' probation. She also gave him a serious tongue-lashing and hinted that if there's a next time for Rich, he might not be so lucky.

Were truer words ever spoken? A few months later, on April 6, 1991, Rich was arrested in the San Fernando Valley on suspicion of burglary. The sad odyssey began when Rich went to a hospital and asked for painkillers. He was turned away and in desperation, reportedly drove to a pharmacy where he used a tire iron to break a window. When he was unable to squeeze in, he smashed another window, this time cutting his arm. Disgusted and in pain, Rich returned to his car and left without taking anything. Police stopped the car several miles away and arrested him. Former costar Dick Van Patten paid the $5,000 to bail Adam out of jail; the case is still pending.

Rusty Nailed

Danny Bonaduce and Adam Rich are relatively lucky: at least they're still alive. One of the most famous child stars in TV history wasn't so fortunate.

Rusty Hamer was born on February 15, 1947, in Tenafly, New Jersey. His family moved to Los Angeles in 1951, and with no acting experience beyond a single amateur play, he went to an open audition for *The Danny Thomas Show.* Thomas hired the outgoing boy, and Rusty played Danny's smart-aleck son Rusty Williams on the show for its entire run, from 1953 to 1964.

"Rusty was only five and a half years old when I first got to know him," Thomas said, and they got very close very fast due to tragic circumstances: within months of the start of filming, Rusty's father, a shirt salesman, died of cancer. Thomas recalled, "One day while we were on the set, I saw a tear in his eye. He turned to me and said, 'You're the only daddy I've got left.' " Thomas held the boy tightly and the two of them had a good, long cry.

Rusty was seventeen when the show went off the air. A large share of his income had gone to supporting the Hamer family, and another big lump of it was lost when a mutual fund went belly-up. For a while, he survived on what was left while waiting for another role to come along. But, like so many others who had been closely identified with a part, he was unable to get work. That troubled him, because he "found the real world a very hard place."

Just *how* hard no one knew until 1966, when Rusty was rushed to Santa Monica Emergency Hospital with a .22 caliber bullet lodged in his abdomen. The wound was listed as accidental, but few in the industry believed that. Tongues wagged and everyone felt sorry for the young man—but no one gave him *work*.

Rusty stayed in town for a year after that where, as his older brother John puts it, "He squandered most of [his money]." Finally, he moved to De Ridder, Louisiana, where John and their mother lived. His money was now completely gone and, to survive, Rusty worked as a messenger, a newspaper delivery-man, an offshore oil rigger, a house painter, and a short-order cook in John's restaurant. He lived in a trailer in a rustic section of town.

Rusty went back to Hollywood in 1970 for what he hoped would be a comeback, costarring in the new series *Make Room for Granddaddy*. But the show failed quickly; a marriage was equally short-lived, lasting just a year, and Rusty returned to De Ridder more despondent than ever.

"Over the years," says John, "[Rusty] grew more and more into a loner." And a quirky one at that: eventually packing 240 pounds on his five-foot eight-inch frame, Rusty rarely bathed, wore the same blue coveralls day after day, and grew a long beard that was always unkempt. "He was overweight, and tormented that Hollywood had rejected him," says John. Rusty became even more depressed in recent years when his mother took ill, and in 1989 a chronic back condition made it difficult for the forty-two-year-old to work or enjoy his favorite pastime, fishing. Emotionally, he deteriorated rapidly.

The strange behavior continued. He didn't want to look at himself anymore, so he put a sheet over the mirror in his trailer. On New Year's Eve, he climbed out of his truck, tripped over a tree trunk, whipped out a gun, and shot the stump. Just over a week later, a neighbor found him roaming around outside the trailer, naked except for a blanket and carrying the gun. He could be heard babbling incoherently for days thereafter, and although the neighbor called the sheriff, there was nothing anyone could do to help the young man.

On January 17, Rusty went to town, entered a shop, and announced that he was going to shoot himself that night. No one believed him; they thought he was just being wacky Rusty. But he fooled them. Later that day, when no one was around to hear, Rusty Hamer put a .357 magnum to his head and pulled the trigger. John discovered his body the next day: beside it was a photo a fan had sent to be autographed, a picture of Rusty from *Make Room for Daddy*.

"Rusty was basically bitter and disillusioned about life," John says. "He was unhappy. But when he wasn't, he was a very dependable, very loving and very warm man."

Amazing what TV Babylon can do to good people.

Yet, some good came of Rusty's death. At the same

time, fellow child star Jay North, TV's *Dennis the Menace* from 1959 to 1963, also found himself headed down the path to self-destruction. Unemployable in the industry and working in a health food store, he says, "I was addicted to caffeine," and admits that he was guzzling twelve cans of Dr Pepper (now *that's* a Pepper) and up to nine cups of coffee a day. He was also "addicted to nasal sprays, which have amphetamines in them."

Wired from the caffeine, Jay would fly into rages due to even small provocations, and became so paranoid about people being "out to get me" that, by the end of 1989, he refused to budge from his apartment.

Shortly thereafter, he learned of Rusty's death and realized that he was headed in the same direction. If not for Rusty, said the thirty-seven-year-old, "I wouldn't have realized just how bad I was and I probably would have committed suicide myself." Instead, a few days later, he went to see a doctor and learned that he had an overactive adrenal gland. The doctor put him on medication, and Jay eliminated caffeine from his life. Since then, the persecution delusions and anger have left.

"I feel I have a life again," Jay says.

Rusty Hamer may have died tragically, but at least he didn't die in vain. And sometimes, that's as generous as TV Babylon gets.

LA Loss

David Rappaport had a lot going for him.

The thirty-nine-year-old English actor was working steadily on television and in the movies, a not inconsiderable feat. Most prominently, Rappaport had starred in the film *Time Bandits* (1981) and in the TV series *The Wizard* in 1986. He also had a recurring, high-profile role in *L.A. Law* as ruthless British attorney Hamilton Schuyler, a nemesis of Victor Sifuentes (Jimmy Smits).

What was amazing about Rappaport's achievements was that he only stood three feet, eleven inches tall. He may not have been as famous as Herve Villechaize, the *Fantasy Island* star who stands an inch shorter, but Rappaport worked a lot more.

Despite his success, Rappaport wasn't happy. For one thing, a proposed spinoff featuring a character he'd played on the series *Hooperman* went nowhere. Ditto plans for a series featuring Hamilton Schuyler. For another, he wanted roles that didn't in *some* way allude to his height: he wanted to be considered for parts because he was a good actor, not because he was a dwarf. That wasn't happening and, on principle, it depressed him terribly.

Perhaps more significantly, Rappaport regarded his personal life as a shambles. His ten-year-long marriage to normal-sized college girlfriend, Jane, ended in 1985, and his relationship with stunning Eliza Lende was at a standstill. Reportedly, Eliza insisted that he do something about his depression—something of which Rappaport was incapable. He had an artist's temperament, and those who know him say that much of his creative passion came from anger and brooding.

The final blow was the AIDS-related death of a friend who lived down the street from Rappaport's $1.5-million Hollywood home. The two were very close, and his deterioration weighed heavily on the actor. Prior to his death, the man had tried to kill himself by hosing carbon monoxide into his car. He was found and revived, and lived a few weeks more before AIDS claimed him.

To Rappaport, the attempt had seemed a dignified and painless way to escape the inevitable. In his friend's case, it was death by AIDS. In his own case, it was a lonely future filled with parts he didn't want.

"I look at boring people every day," he said shortly before his death, "and I say, 'God, I wish I could be like that,' but my lot is to be unique, special, so I have to put up with it." However, he added pointedly, "It's a hard life."

Too hard to bear, as it turned out.

On the night of March 4, 1990, Rappaport got in his white, 1982 Volkswagen convertible, drove to an isolated spot on a dirt road below the famous HOLLY-

Actor David Rappaport in 1985. (AP/Wide World, Jim Mulqueen)

WOOD sign, and ran a hose from the tailpipe into the back window. He used tape to close the space around the open window, then lay down on the back seat to go to sleep . . . permanently.

Within minutes, a friend, Rose Berger, happened to drive by. Spotting the car, Rose went to the nearby ranch she managed and phoned police. A squad car arrived quickly. Rappaport was no longer breathing when the police arrived, and the officer performed cardiopulmonary resuscitation. By the time paramedics got there, the actor had regained consciousness and was taken to the Queen of Angels-Hollywood Presbyterian Medical Center, where he was hospitalized for several days.

After the suicide attempt, Rappaport was persuaded, finally, to see a psychiatrist. But there was simply no getting around the problems that had caused him to try to take his life. And now there was another problem, more immediate and distressing. Every actor who stars in a series or film has to be insured. If they die during shooting, and the project has to be scrapped, the producer is covered. Because of what he'd done, Rappaport could not be easily insured. That meant he'd have trouble getting *any* kind of part that required a lengthy shooting schedule.

During the next few months, Rappaport spent most of his time at home with his Labrador Rickie (named after singer Rickie Lee Jones), or visiting with his cousin and manager Frankie Leigh. There was no work in his life, and no romance, and he struggled to find a reason why he should go on living.

On May 2, he told Leigh that he was going to drive somewhere and walk the dog. Frankie thought a walk was a good idea; if nothing else, it would get him out of the house. What she didn't know was that he was armed with a .38 caliber revolver.

The actor put Rickie in the car and headed into the Hollywood Hills. Stopping in Laurel Canyon Park, he locked the animal in the car, walked a few paces to a row of bushes, put the gun to his chest, and pulled the trigger. He died instantly.

When Rappaport didn't return home after several hours, Frankie called the police and reported him missing. He wasn't found until 6:00 P.M. the following day, when a jogger noticed his body in the bushes and used a car phone to notify police.

Eliza accompanied Rappaport's body back to England, where he was buried.

David Rappaport never gave a performance that wasn't first rate, and that's the real heartbreaker: although his expectation for greater recognition was unrealistic, Rappaport's faith in his abilities was not misplaced.

It's a shame he never realized how highly regarded he really was.

Gunning for Trouble

When someone takes his or her own life, that's sad. But when they take someone with them, sad becomes heinous. Such was the case with TV actor Albert Salmi and his wife Roberta.

Salmi had a long and successful stage and film career before he began accepting parts on TV. A gun buff and macho western man (even though he was born in Coney Island, New York), Salmi appeared largely in western series, usually as a heavy; his credits include *Wagon Train*, *Bonanza*, *Gunsmoke*, *Have Gun Will Travel*, *Rawhide*, *A Man Called Shenandoah*, *The Virginian*, as well as nonwestern series like *The Twilight Zone*. He was perhaps best known for his continuing roles as Fess Parker's sidekick Yadkin in *Daniel Boone* and Pete in *Petrocelli*.

Despite a fruitful career, Salmi was increasingly unhappy during the past few years. He loved making westerns, but hardly anyone was making them anymore. Because of that, he embraced more and more

the kind of life they exemplified: hard-drinking rugged individualism for men, helpless subservience for
women—stereotypes that were almost as dead as the
Old West itself. He also took comfort in guns, shooting and collecting them, and in other outdoor sports,
especially skiing.

The actor was working, but not on the kinds of
projects he enjoyed. In 1980, after making the film
St. Helens in Washington State, he decided to move
to Spokane with his wife of over twenty years and
their two daughters. But even that rugged environment wasn't enough to make him happy, and he began
to drink a lot. Not only did he yell at Roberta more
and more, he started hitting her as well. As far back
as 1984 he knew he was courting disaster when he
said, "As you get older, parts are fewer and you take
it out on your family, your wife." He wanted to stop,
but he couldn't. Roberta put up with it because she
always hoped a part would come along to snap him
out of it, or that he would change. She held out special
hope in 1988 when he did a pilot called *B-Men*, an *A-
Team* retread; but it failed to sell, and Salmi hit rock
bottom.

By the end of 1989, the actor was drinking half a
bottle of hard liquor a day and beating his wife. Once,
she said, he "began shaking me violently. He hit me
on my breasts, strangled me and pulled my hair." The
fifty-five-year-old woman stuck it out until February
4, at which point she phoned her husband from a hotel
and told him she wanted a divorce. The next day, in
the company of two police detectives, she went back
to the house to collect her things. Salmi wasn't there,
having gone to stay at their condominium in Idaho—
but he'd left behind notes that read, "War of the

Roses. You're a stupid girl. You're living out your picture fantasy," and "We had a good thing going, too bad you tripped in the final straightaway." Roberta hired a detective to watch her and the house, but she had to let him go early in April when her funds ran out.

Sometime during the night of April 22, Salmi returned to the house, unannounced. His wife was alone. They apparently argued, after which Roberta turned and tried to get out of the house; drawing a .25 caliber pistol, her husband fired two bullets into her back as she ran through the kitchen. After making sure she was dead, he went upstairs, took out a powerful Colt .45, and blew a huge hole in his chest.

On Monday, concerned about not having seen Roberta for two days, a neighbor went to the house to check on her. The body was clearly visible through the kitchen window, and the neighbor phoned police.

It would be an oversimplification to say that Roberta died because she loved a man who loved another—the parts he'd played on TV. But the fate of Roberta and Albert Salmi is nonetheless a testimony to the seductive power of TV Babylon.

Natural Causes

Not all deaths in TV Babylon are intentional.

Joan Collins's discovery, twenty-six-year-old Jon-Erik Hexum had a spectacular future ahead of him. After starring in the flop TV series *Voyages* in 1982, Hexum was tapped to star opposite Collins in the TV movie *The Making of a Male Model*. He was a hit, and he and Joan became an off-camera item. Though Joan wasn't able to get him onto *Dynasty* as her lover Dexter (Michael Nader got the part), he landed a starring role in the action series *Cover Up*.

The role of Mac Harper was perfect for Hexum, that of a glib model who's actually a secret agent. Hexum, himself, was a dashing rogue and prankster, qualities that cost him his life. Shortly after the series began shooting, Hexum was clowning around on the set and foolishly put a prop gun to his head. He pulled the trigger. Even though the gun was only loaded with blanks—a charge packed with cotton—the detonation, at that range, was sufficient to shatter his skull and drive bone fragments into his brain. He died not long after going into a coma.

Not all deaths in TV Babylon are explicable.

Possibly the most bizarre death was that of forty-one-year-old Northern J. Calloway, who starred as David, Mr. Hooper's clerk, on *Sesame Street*. In 1980, after six years on the show, Calloway suddenly snapped. He attacked a woman with a pipe and then ran naked down the street, pausing only to eat grass. He was treated for manic depression, and went back to *Sesame Street* for another ten years before finally leaving the show. Shortly thereafter, he went haywire again and was taken to Stoney Ledge Hospital in Ossining, New York: almost as soon as he got there, he passed out and was rushed to Phelps Memorial Hospital, where he died.

Asked to explain the actor's death, a hospital representative said mysteriously, "I can't say anything at all about this case. We've been instructed not to speak." Though natural causes were eventually blamed, an underlying drug problem was suspected. It's a sad state of affairs when not even *Sesame Street* is above contamination.

Because of their celebrity, actors who die in TV Babylon get a great deal of attention. The same is true for actors who take ill. Because these people come into our homes on a regular basis, we feel for them much as we'd feel for family—especially if there's a protracted illness involved.

For five years, Dick York was the bumbling Darrin Stephens on the hit series *Bewitched*. He'd have played the part for three years more, but he retired in 1969 and was replaced by Dick Sargent: an old back injury made it impossible for him to work (nor did his addiction to painkillers and alcohol help matters). He says, "I left in an ambulance writhing in pain, but I never regretted the decision to leave."

Since then, York appeared on TV only three times and, since 1985, he has lived in Rockford, Michigan, literally unable to leave the house: a lifetime of smoking left the horribly emaciated actor so weak that he can only breathe via tubes running from his nose to an oxygen tank.

It's a pathetic fate for a man who seemed so energetic on the tube. Yet, that isn't the only illusion which was propagated by TV—a medium of lies.

A Bee in Her Bonet

Talk about being different from the character you play: no one has been more of a surprise than pretty, seemingly soft-spoken Lisa Bonet. Like Bill Cosby's real-life daughter, his TV daughter has raised a few ruckuses of her own, usually in tandem with her husband, rock musician Lenny Kravitz.

Lisa and Lenny first met at a New Edition concert in 1985, when Lisa was seventeen and Kravitz was twenty. They married in 1988 and have a daughter, Zoe.

Because of her work on one of the top-rated shows on TV, Bonet is fair grist for the mills of paparazzi and reporters. Neither she nor her husband like that: "It's a real fucked up way to make a living," Lenny has decided, "by following people around and taking pictures and writing bad things about them."

But "bad things" is a pretty subjective label, and if Kravitz doesn't like reading about how he or his wife swung or kicked at someone, they shouldn't lose their cool.

Lisa had a run-in with a photographer in 1988, when she went over and kicked him in the leg. But she and her husband outdid themselves on December 22, 1989, engaging in a battle that won Lisa the epithet "Rambo-mom" in the tabloid *Star*.

Autograph hound Michael Wehrmann, twenty-three, and twenty-eight-year-old photographer Angela Coqueran—who has been highly successful at snapping celebrity candids—had gone to JFK airport in

Lisa Bonet, age sixteen—young and unjaded—at the start of her tenure on *The Cosby show*. (© NBC-TV)

New York to try and get pictures of singer Michael Jackson, who was scheduled to be arriving there. They were in luck: Jackson showed up and "was friendly," Wehrmann recalls. He "even took off his sunglasses while we took pictures."

As the two were leaving, Wehrmann spotted Bonet. Zoe was in her arms, Kravitz walking a few steps ahead of them; the three were headed to a gate to board a plane for the Bahamas.

The two fans stopped in their tracks, whipped out their cameras, and snapped one shot apiece.

Suddenly spotting the duo, Lisa shouted, "No pictures! I said no pictures!" as though she were an expert on Constitutional law and it was her decision to make.

Not wishing to cause a scene, Michael hurriedly slipped his camera into his coat pocket. Before Angela could cap her own lens, Lenny lunged at her. Angela says, "The first thing I knew Lenny was pushing me and grabbing my wrist and twisting it, trying to grab my camera." Naturally, she resisted.

When Lenny realized that he was losing it, he angrily threw aside the carry-on bag he'd been holding, and backed away. Then, like tag-team fighters, Lisa charged. She came at Michael and kicked his groin with her hard, pointy western boot. Though Michael turned to avoid the kick, he wasn't fast enough. A witness later told a reporter that Bonet kicked the lanky fan "so hard it made a loud noise."

"I let out a muffled scream of agony," Wehrmann says. He fell to the floor and "saw black" for about twenty seconds. However, he heard Lisa swearing and, afraid she was going to attack again, he got up with Angela's help and backed off.

While the two photographers huddled together, Lenny huffily grabbed his bag and walked toward the gate with Lisa. Suddenly, the musician tossed down the bag again and, swearing, stalked back to where Wehrmann was standing.

Wehrmann recalls, "He put his face about four inches from mine and began shouting, 'You have to respect the lady!'" Calling Michael "scum," Lenny returned to where Lisa and Zoe were standing and boarded the plane.

In terrible pain, Wehrmann left the airport and went to the hospital. There were bruises but no serious damage. After reflecting on the incident, Michael and Angela decided to file a complaint with the police. A warrant was issued for Bonet's arrest on third-degree assault; Kravitz was charged with harassment. Nearly a week later, the photographers filed a suit against the couple, demanding $4 million for assault and another $20 million in punitive damages. As their attorney Harry Lipsig explains the case, "The point of punitive damages is to teach the wrongdoer not to do it again."

Both the civil and criminal lawsuits are pending. In the meantime, as soon as he got back from holiday, Kravitz continued to promote his new record. "Its title? *Let Love Rule.*

Stars want it both ways: they want the fame and the money, and presume that all they're required to give up in return is their performance. That isn't so. When viewers like an actor, it's because they have certain charisma or charm, an endearing manner, or just good old physical attractiveness. TV keeps them slightly remote; the chance to experience these qualities briefly, in person, is something few fans can resist. Celebrities who don't understand this should consider another profession.

Kick boxing, perhaps.

In Sickness, Health, and Unemployment

A number of stars treat their fans without respect or gratitude, but some of them treat each other even worse.

Married actors usually experience one of two extremes. If everyone's working, things are usually peachy—witness Michael Tucker and Jill Eikenberry of *L.A. Law*, Patricia Wettig and Ken Olin of *thirtysomething*, and many others. If one's working and the other isn't—watch out.

David Birney was thirty-three, Meredith Baxter twenty-five, when they first met on the set of their costarring series, *Bridget Loves Bernie* (1972). Baxter was an easygoing, self-described "Pollyanna" who was a graduate of Michigan's Interlochen Arts Academy, and had previously guest-starred on TV shows like *The Interns* and *The Young Lawyers*. Birney was (and still is) a "passionate" stage actor who also costarred in the soap *Love Is a Many Splendored Thing*. When the two met, Baxter was newly

divorced and the mother of two small children; they
married in 1974.

Though both worked in TV, their careers went in
very different directions. Birney, who can play comedy or drama with great skill, is one of the industry's
most underrated stars. When *Bridget Loves Bernie*
went off the air after a single season, he repeatedly
grabbed for—and just missed—the brass ring in a succession of shows: *Serpico* (1976), as the tough detective; *St. Elsewhere* (1983), as the sex-starved Dr. Ben
Samuels; and *Glitter* (1984), as a reporter for a *People*-like magazine. Birney's performances in all these
shows were always on the money, even though the
characters or shows failed to click.

Baxter, meanwhile, starred in two hit series: *Family*
(1976–1980) and *Family Times* (1982–1989). The shows
were successful, but the characters were bland and she
rarely got to stretch her abilities.

The irony couldn't have been lost on the actors: one
was doing good work but was frustrated because the
shows were failing; the other was giving week after
week of similar, pedestrian performances, frustrated
because she was hamstrung by the formula that made
each show work.

Baxter once said, partly in jest, that "Attila the Hun
is more low-key than David." That intensity is what
helps give Birney's performances their fascinating
edge. In order to be near Meredith during a very difficult pregnancy, David accepted the starring role in
Glitter, which he describes as "hardly the artistic backbone of my life." But at least it kept him in Southern
California. After the birth of their twins Peter and
Molly in 1984, however, there was *more* tension in the
household. The failure of *Glitter* contributed to that;

so did David's time away from home, which included virtually back-to-back stints as Salieri in *Amadeus* on Broadway, a lengthy shoot of a miniseries *Master of the Game* in Africa, and another Broadway run, as a frustrated architect in *Benefactors*.

"It's a schizophrenic life," he said. "I have a home with a wife and children, yet I'm frequently away from them." When he *was* home, his wife would work long hours: she'd get up at 5:45 each morning and be in bed at 9 every evening, leaving little time to repair any rifts that appeared in the relationship. (During Meredith's pregnancy with the twins, the couple was so busy that one night they had to do their Lamaze practice by phone.)

Meredith said that when problems would arise—for example, David "obsessing" about his work—she'd always "try to remember during fights or difficult times . . . 'What's at stake here?' " She said, half-jokingly, "That's probably the reason we continue having children. Even when you're going through a rough time you can always think back to those kids. I know the kids have seen David and me when we're not talking to each other. The tension is high. But then next week, we're okay."

After a while, however, things no longer returned to being okay. In addition to the time they spent apart, there was money. A hit TV series pays lots of it, the stage very little. No matter how much a couple may be in love, actors are by nature competitive. And although David was proud of his stage work, there was no way he could compete with his wife financially.

In public, Baxter and Birney put on happy faces. In private, however, the relationship was spiraling downward fast. The actress later said that in private, David "inflicted physical violence on me. At least on one occasion I was forced to seek medical attention because of it."

By February of 1989 the pressure had become too much for her to handle and she filed for divorce. In her complaint she noted that Birney "has been emotionally abusive of me on a regular basis in front of the children, calling me derogatory names and sneering at and deriding my abilities as a mother and homemaker. His physical disciplining of the children borders on abuse."

That's her view: you wouldn't expect divorce papers to say anything else. The truth is, she was working long hours: even if she wanted to be Harriet Homemaker, when would she have had the time? And there are parents who feel that any kind of physical discipline is abuse. As for calling her derogatory names, Baxter never tells what names those were. Does "dummy" qualify? In the intentionally, misleadingly vague world of divorce lawyer lingo, it does.

The truth is, Birney's heart is good, and when the divorce and ensuing publicity starting hitting the tabloids, he issued a statement that addressed her hurtful remarks: "It is not uncommon for a parent to act out anger over divorce through the children and in the custody process. I believe that this process should be private. I have been deeply saddened by Meredith's allegations and the impact, given their public nature, both upon the children's welfare and upon my good name." Privately, he said that there was one thing he regretted above all: that "this situation involves children whose lives are at risk of exposure, of emotional damage." Everything else seemed trivial to him compared to that, and both he and Meredith resolved to end the matter as swiftly and quietly as possible. In the end, the couple settled upon joint custody of the children.

Regardless of who was at fault, it doesn't take much imagination to figure out how different the actors' lives might have been if TV didn't eat up so many of her hours and so few of his. The medium itself isn't to blame, but the extremes of success and failure it creates generate stresses that few relationships can survive.

Remarkably similar to David Birney's situation is that of former film headliner Ryan O'Neal. Since 1980, Ryan has been living with TV superstar Farrah Fawcett, whose career has far overshadowed his. Never mind that her own film career was a disaster: she's managed to star in some very distinguished TV movies, such as *The Burning Bed* (1984) and *Margaret Bourke-White* (1989). Through these, she's gained credibility as an actress, and good TV roles have not been wanting. But Ryan—

A series of film stinkers put him in the commercial doghouse; that, and his inability to maintain a stable relationship with his older kids (Tatum from first wife Joanna Moore, Griffin and Patrick from second wife Leigh Taylor-Young) have made him susceptible to what Farrah describes as "mood swings."

Irresponsibility has a lot to do with his problems as well. When he and Farrah fell in love, Ryan simply up-and-moved out of his house and into hers, leaving his kids in the care of a housekeeper. Griffin recalls, "One day, without warning, he came home and said, 'This is it, guys. You're on your own.'" Tatum, then sixteen, apparently never forgave him for that; when

Farrah Fawcett at the start of her career, as one of the original *Charlie's Angels.* (© ABC-TV)

she married tennis star John McEnroe in 1986, neither Ryan nor Farrah was invited.

As for violence, Ryan's outbursts have included such treats as throwing a pool cue at Farrah ("It struck the wall about two feet above Farrah's head and stuck in the drywall," Griffin says) and apparently throwing punches at her (Griffin says he has "seen Farrah with bruised ribs, red slap marks on her pretty face and a cast on her wrist, all due to fights with Ryan").

However, Ryan's pièce de résistance occurred in 1984. After breaking Griffin's nose twice on separate occasions, he knocked out several of the boy's teeth during an argument.

"I punched him, and his teeth exploded," Ryan says. "It was horrible."

How nice of him to notice.

Since that attack, Ryan has made keeping his temper a top priority in his life—even more important than his career. And so far, he's apparently been succeeding. This has been particularly true since the birth of his and Farrah's son Redmond in 1985. Farrah and Ryan have also had no problem acting together on their sitcom *Good Sports*, in which they played TV sportscasters with a like-hate relationship. With any luck, Redmond won't grow up to say, as Griffin recently did: "He's a jerk, but I love him very much."

Calling Arnie Becker!

In 1980, while filming the fantasy epic *Clash of the Titans* in England, twenty-nine-year-old star Harry Hamlin (playing the Greek hero Perseus) had a fling with costar Ursula Andress (playing the goddess of love, Aphrodite). They had a child, who remained in Europe with his mother while Harry returned to the United States to build a career in Hollywood.

The arrangement seemed civilized, even enlightened: the child visited Harry and vice versa whenever possible, and the couple lived like an amicable divorcé and divorcée, even though they'd never been married. Harry just wasn't the marrying kind, it seemed—and maybe he should have stayed that way.

In 1986, after five years of having not much to do, the actor was tapped to play (of all things) the morally upright attorney Michael Kuzak in the new series *L.A. Law*. The show was a hit, and Harry was an even bigger hit: *People* magazine went so far as to name him its sexiest man of the year.

That same year Harry married his lover of two years, actress Laura Johnson who, since 1983, had been starring as ex-hooker Terry Hartford on *Falcon Crest*. "This is the man I'm gonna stay with," Laura said at the time, a song in her voice and stars in her eyes.

Jump to September of 1989: Hamlin files for divorce. He cites the tired catchall "irreconcilable differences," though privately he's come to the conclusion that Laura is "a monster and a shrew." Not so coinciden-

Harry Hamlin and Laura Johnson in April of 1985, a week after their wedding. Before long, the smiles would fade . . . (UPI/Bettmann)

tally, during the previous spring he'd worked with twenty-five-year-old beauty Nicollette Sheridan on the appropriately titled film *Deceptions* (referred to by some critics as *L.A. Raw*), and had fallen in love with her.

Initially, Harry and Laura were going to be as civil as Harry and Ursula. They were going to share their $1.6-million Beverly Hills home until they could come to terms on property. However, the good intentions soured when Hamlin apparently decided that he wanted the house for himself and Nicollette. As Laura stated in legal papers filed in Los Angeles on February 9, "Harry's harassment and emotional abuse of me has caused me great emotional trauma and adversely affected my ability to obtain work."

The specifics read as though they came straight from the film *War of the Roses*. Excerpts, describing some of Harry's activities from October 1989, to January 1990, include:

• "I was sitting in my bedroom and Harry, who had been hiding in the closet, came out, walked across my room and called me an asshole. A few days after that, Harry again repeated this performance while I was on the telephone. When I realized Harry was again hiding in the closest eavesdropping, I made an effort to ignore him."

• "Harry came into my bedroom and insisted on playing videotapes of himself from *L.A. Law* over and over while I was making final notes on a script and dressing for a meeting."

• "I learned that Harry's girlfriend Nicollette Sheridan had been in my bedroom, bath and closets while I was out of town. When I confronted Harry about this, he said, 'I have no control over

Nicollette when she is in this house.' [When] I yelled at Harry, rather than trying to calm me [he] even took out his tape recorder to try to record my emotional breakdown because he said it would help in the divorce case."

• As she was leaving the house one day, Laura says, "Harry yelled at me saying, 'You are a slut, a whore, you have been fucking around for years, and I'm going to tell everyone in the industry what kind of a person you really are.' " Afterwards, she says, "he tried to chase me down the driveway."

• During December, when a producer was visiting her at the house, Harry allegedly said, "This is the first Christmas that Laura has been sober enough to decorate a tree."

• Harry turned on music "full blast without regard to the fact that I am usually studying scripts."

There's more, most of it of the same goading, spiteful nature. How much of it was true, and how much of it was Laura's embittered impressions, cannot be determined. And in deference to Harry, it should be pointed out that while Laura was earning close to $200,000 a year on her own—admittedly shy of Harry's $1.3 million, but not bad at all—she was asking for $15,000 a month in spousal support (including $500 for "facials and hair"), which seemed somewhat excessive to Harry.

Meanwhile, Laura privately admitted that to Hamlin's credit, "there were private matters which Harry could have made public, which would have been upsetting to me . . . and I appreciate and respect his integrity for keeping private matters private."

Still, the extensive newspaper and magazine publication of Laura's complaint was enough to get Hamlin to the bargaining table, and on March 9, Harry, Laura, and their attorneys sat down for an eight-hour meeting to hammer out details of a settlement. The house was to be sold, from which Laura would get $700,000. She'd also be paid $250,000 as her half of their savings, $200,000 from their retirement fund, and $5,000 a month alimony.

Though the matter was ended, there's a wicked irony to the entire affair. Hamlin met Nicollette because she did *Deceptions*. Yet, she never would have gotten the part if another actress hadn't turned it down.

That actress was Laura Johnson.

Second Banana Split

Battered egos, falling out of love, drugs, and drink—
these are the common causes of marital unhappiness
and divorce in TV Babylon. However, the divorce of
Ed and Victoria McMahon is in a class by itself.

Here's a gentle and good man, despite the ribbing
he takes on *The Tonight Show* for drinking (he doesn't
go to the excesses described by Johnny Carson; no
one could). It's no coincidence that the sixty-seven-
year-old McMahon started out in TV playing a clown
on the variety show *Big Top:* in person, he's a trust-
worthy man who wouldn't hurt a soul. (Unless it's an
enemy of his country: McMahon fought in both World
War II and Korea, as a fighter pilot. In fact, the man
deserves credit for more than courage: how many bat-
tle-hardened vets would feel comfortable putting on a
big false nose and red wig? McMahon's self-image is
beyond reproach.)

It's appropriate for one other reason that McMahon
began his career playing a clown. Through no fault of

his own, his divorce from Victoria was more public and circus-like, with more sideshows, than any of the divorces of his friend Mr. Carson. (An ironic footnote: McMahon first teamed with Johnny Carson on the daytime game show *Who Do You Trust?* in 1958. The professional relationship has lasted longer than any of their marriages.)

Ed and forty-four-year-old Victoria, a former airline stewardess, had been married for thirteen years when he discovered that Victoria was having an ongoing affair with thirty-three-year-old Beverly Hills police officer Kieron Foley, who she'd met at a local anticrime lecture. What seems a bizarre coupling on the surface—the rich woman and the boy-cop—makes sense when you consider that Foley lifts weights and has an almost compulsive sense of adventure, qualities that clearly distinguish him from the more hearth-and-home-oriented McMahon. Qualities that obviously appealed to Victoria.

The circus got underway when Ed filed for divorce on July 25, 1989. The press reported that he'd cut his wife's allowance to $2,500 (one-tenth of what she was accustomed to), canceled her credit cards, and fired the household help. He also changed the name of his yacht from *Victoria* to *Miss Katherine*, after the couple's three-year-old adopted daughter. What seemed petty on the surface (and especially in the tabloids) was actually indicative of how deeply Ed was hurt.

But if Victoria was hurting, she didn't show it. While McMahon did what he had to do and nursed his wounds, his wife flitted about like a teen with a driver's license. That's not unusual in situations like these, but because the press dotes on Hollywood the situation degenerated from merely unfortunate to

The calm before the storm. Ed McMahon, wife Victoria, and cat Ruffy in 1986. (AP/Wide World)

colossally tawdry. There was ongoing photographic coverage of Victoria with Foley in public and—in an obvious dig—modeling clothes alongside Johnny Carson's ex-wife Joanna at a charity function. The circus got a new ring when she went to Hawaii with her new beau, leaving Katherine with her devoted father.

The mess ended up in court in late October, and though McMahon was delighted that he and Victoria would be sharing custody of Katherine, he was ordered to pay his ex-wife $50,000 each month, tax free, while proceeds from their home—the $6-million mansion in Beverly Hills—would be divided equally. In September, the terms hammered out for the entire estate put the matter to rest. The one catch: the divorce wouldn't become final until January 1, 1991, since the couple wanted to file a joint tax return for the year. Even in divorce, it's sometimes advisable to continue sharing *certain* sheets.

McMahon bought a $2.5-million Beverly Hills home, and planned to live there when he marries blond, forty-eight-year-old restaurant manager Joanna Ford. In a wonderfully old-fashioned romantic flourish, he proposed to his old friend on national TV, during a live broadcast of the Hollywood Christmas Parade. Unfortunately, it was not in the cards for McMahon to find contentment with Ms. Ford. In December of 1990, just a few weeks before the couple's planned January 12 wedding date, McMahon called it off. The decision apparently was triggered when McMahon found himself arguing with his fiancée about certain pieces of furniture Victoria was supposed to get. If things were tense before the marriage, McMahon could just imagine what they'd be like afterward! Rather than find himself trapped in a tense or unpleasant relationship, he simply canceled the wedding. Whether they get back together again remains to be seen. At the moment, McMahon says he's at peace with his life and his daughter and sees no reason to play games with what is finally a happy and peaceful lifestyle.

Enterprising Actor

Going to court for a divorce is one thing. But being a married man sued for palimony by not one but *two* women is something else altogether. In that respect, boldly going where few men have gone before was *Star Trek*'s Captain Kirk. Fifty-eight-year-old William Shatner ended up with not one but two suits, back-to-back.

Shatner has been married to his forty-four-year-old second-wife Marcy for sixteen years. Marcy is an attractive woman known to televiewers from her co-starring role in Shatner's immortal Promise margarine commercials.

Ironically, it was Marcy who got the ball rolling, so to speak: she was the one who hired thirty-year-old former model and aspiring screenwriter Eva-Marie Friedrick, in August of 1986, to work as her assistant. In just a few months, Eva-Marie was also working as Shatner's assistant.

According to very pretty Eva-Marie, William Shatner

promised that she "wouldn't be stuck behind a desk and . . . would learn to become a producer." Several months after that, says Eva-Marie, they became lovers. Shatner also reportedly promised her a role in the unbearably awful *Star Trek V*, which he directed.

The young woman maintains that Shatner lost inter-

William Shatner, who has had to deal with a pair of kiss-and-tell suits. So far, Yaka—pictured here—has not pressed for palimony. (AP/Wide World)

est in her in October of 1988, concurrent with her being severely injured in a car accident. He fired her in November, after which—she claims—he would dial her home phone and hang up when she answered. Why? Eva-Marie says it was to harass her.

On December 26, 1989, feeling as though she'd been betrayed, Eva-Marie filed papers in California Superior Court in Los Angeles, which charged the actor with fraud, breach of contract, violation of state labor laws, negligence, and both intentional and negligent infliction of emotional distress.

Shatner's response: "Her lawsuit is totally unjustified. She was never under contract and was dismissed for valid reasons." He didn't elaborate, and he wasn't terribly concerned. Until two weeks later.

On January 4, another claim was filed against Shatner: this time it was a $3-million palimony suit, handled by palimony pro Marvin Mitchelson on behalf of voluptuous thirty-four-year-old actress Vira Montes.

Montes says that she had an affair with Shatner that lasted six years, during which time she was his "companion, confidante, and homemaker." Montes says that he had promised to divorce Marcy and marry her, and she notes, "I don't know how he could have paid any attention to his wife anyway. He'd tell her he was having to stay late at the studio . . . but really he would race around to see me." She says they would make love, after which he'd beam back home "in time for dinner."

Shatner's response to this one: "The case she presents is ridiculous. She was a friend whom I tried to help. Someone obviously got to her and convinced her that she could possibly make a killing by suing me."

In any case, Marcy has stuck by her husband, and

it looks as though Shatner has dodged a pair of Phaser beams.

The suits went nowhere, but making a triptych of woes for Shatner in 1989, he was also involved in litigation over one of the horses he owns in a farm west of Lexington, Kentucky. Appropriately enough, the suit also involved sex—horse sex—and a breeding agreement Shatner allegedly had with another Lexington horse owner. Shatner won that one too: he didn't have to allow his prize stallion to mate with the other owner's mares. It isn't known whether Marcy looked into setting up any similar arrangements.

Johnny Get Your Checkbook, and Other Tales

When it comes to men and divorce, some men have longer battles, some have messier battles, and some have more battles. Yet, because of his monologue jokes about the subject, no one is more synonymous with marital discord than Ed McMahon's boss, sixty-four-year-old Johnny Carson.

Not only did Carson go through three divorces, but he holds a record for longevity: the first one returned to vex him in April of 1990, twenty-seven years after the papers were signed!

Johnny was married to Joan "Jody" Carson—the mother of his three children—from 1949 to 1963. In 1989, aged sixty-three and living in a small hotel, the woman was earning $13,500 a year. That was the sum Carson had agreed to pay her until 1999. But it was less than a drop in the bucket of Carson's annual $40-million income and, through ace divorce lawyer Raoul Felder, she asked for an increase to $120,000.

"I'm like many women of my age with no way of

earning a living," she said. "I don't want to get rich. I am simply forced into this situation."

Carson was served in L.A., and Felder says, "Carson refused to accept service, but my man touched him with the papers. Carson let them fall to the ground."

They might have remained there, for all the good the suit did. Upon reviewing the case, Justice Phyllis Gangel-Jacob found what she described as a "little glitch": two weeks after Jody had divorced Carson, she'd wed ad executive Donald Buckley, a union that lasted six years. Carson's fame and wealth notwithstanding, he wasn't really responsible for Jody's upkeep. And it wasn't as though the woman was destitute: she had $400,000 in the bank.

Jody hopped off the gravy train long before it hit top speed, which has to be frustrating to her. That's one reason many wives stay with their husbands in TV Babylon, despite infidelities and other failings.

Many . . . but not all.

Booze for the Villains

Alcohol-related abuse is a common reason for divorce throughout the nation, and TV Babylon is hardly immune. For many, the long periods of idleness between jobs is an invitation to drink. For others, no invitation is needed. They hit the bottle and then, in many cases, they hit their spouses.

Larry Linville starred as the arrogant, ineffective Major Frank Burns on the long-running series *M*A*S*H*. In real life, he's a pleasant enough man . . . when he's sober. On December 28, 1989, the fifty-year-old Larry's fourth wife, thirty-seven-year-old Susan, filed for divorce, claiming that he beat her on more than twenty different occasions during their four years of wedded bliss.

"Throughout our marriage," Susan said in the divorce papers, Larry "has had a serious alcohol problem. Quite often when he drinks, he becomes mean and abusive."

Susan says that the worst of these incidents occurred

in January of 1986, "when he became angry at me in a parking lot in Las Vegas and kicked me fifteen to twenty times about the body, arms, legs and head, literally laying me up in bed for a full week."

Nice guy.

Susan finally had enough when they were in Clearwater, Florida, where Linville was appearing in a play. They had attended a cast Christmas party where the actor is said to have had "in excess of fifteen beers." Back in their room, he accused her of having flirted with the director. Susan says, "I then realized that the look on [his] face was one I had seen many times before and I became quite concerned for my safety inasmuch as this facial expression virtually always signals violent behavior."

Susan charges that Linville then began to shake her violently and called her "a series of filthy names [then] threw me on the floor and ripped my skirt and slip from my body." Then he took the garments and her dog, saying that "he did not want there to be any 'evidence' and that I would never see my dog again."

The dog returned a half hour later, but Larry did not; the next morning, Susan flew to their house in Bradbury, California. She filed for divorce a day after receiving what she categorizes as an "extremely threatening and abusive" phone call from him. In addition to asking for $12,500 a month (Linville earns an average of $24,000 a month), she requested a temporary restraining order to prevent the actor from coming within 100 yards of her. The latter request was granted. The divorce itself is still pending.

Linville's attorney insists that there's been "no violence," just "a lot of deception—and it's all been on her side."

Regardless of who's fudging the facts, this is the illusion-making power of TV Babylon at its best: where else could a man working on divorce number four become famous playing a character who refused to divorce his wife?

Maybe there was something in the air that December: drink was also responsible for striking terror into the heart—and a rift in the marriage—of former *Little House On the Prairie* star, twenty-five-year-old Melissa Gilbert.

Gilbert, whose most famous romantic involvement was with infamous movie actor Rob Lowe, married actor and writer Bo Brinkman in February of 1988. The following May, their son Dakota was born.

Like Linville, Brinkman became upset when he thought his wife was flirting—in this case, with a costar on the TV film *China Nights*, which she was filming in Hong Kong. After drinking heavily, Brinkman threw a tantrum in their hotel, reportedly threatening to kill Melissa or run off with Dakota. Understandably frightened, Melissa grabbed her son and ran out in her bathrobe, then had security personnel working on the film take her to another hotel. Afterward, the guards personally escorted Bo to a plane headed back to the United States. A few days later, the contrite Brinkman checked into a detox center in Los Angeles, aware that the future of his marriage depended upon how much he wanted to save it.

In that respect, the situation is similar to the unstable nine-year-long union of thirty-year-old TV superstar Valerie Bertinelli and her thirty-three-year-old rock star husband Eddie Van Halen.

Eddie Van Halen and wife Valerie Bertinelli. (AP/Wide World)

As in his videos, Eddie's kind of goofy in person, usually grinning and looking either bemused or confused. One is driven to wonder, in his presence, just what's so damn *funny*.

Turns out that nothing is, really. Eddie has a drinking problem, and although he checked into the Betty Ford Center in 1987, together with his brother and band mate Alex, Valerie says, "Ed went for all the wrong reasons. He went into the program because his brother went, not because he really wanted to take care of himself." (He also might have gone because of rumors that while shooting the TV movie *Ordinary*

Heroes in St. George, Utah, a few months before, his distraught wife sought comfort from hunky costar Richard Dean Anderson of *MacGyver*.)

As a result of Eddie's halfhearted effort, Valerie says that Eddie was helped only "for a while." He went back on the bottle, and even though he wasn't abusive to Valerie, neither was he the sensitive man she'd married; he became a smirking space cadet.

Valerie stayed with him because, she says, "I'm addicted to my husband." However, she was afraid he was destroying himself and, In January of 1990, prevailed upon him to enter a drug and alcohol center in Burbank. Concurrently, Valerie attended meetings of Al-Anon, which is devoted to assisting the families of alcoholics. "I feel more sorry for Ed than I do for myself," she said. "If worse comes to worst, I can always pick up and leave, but he's still stuck with his problem."

Eddie seems to have cleaned up his act, and the addition of a son to the fold—Wolfgang, born March 18, 1991—may help to keep him clean. What's significant about this story is that Valerie gave Eddie several chances to turn his life around. That isn't often the case. Witness the split of *Entertainment Tonight*'s pretty Leeza Gibbons and her TV-star husband Chris Quinten.

The thirty-two-year-old Leeza met the star of England's hit soap opera *Coronation Street* late in 1988, and married the fun, charming actor just a few weeks later, on December 10, 1988. Chris moved to L.A., naively expecting to translate his triumphs across the Atlantic to success in Hollywood. It didn't happen—not even with Leeza's help and connections.

A proposed TV series, *Son of Grizzly Adams*, was stillborn, and nothing else even got that close.

Apparently, Chris didn't handle the setbacks very well. Instead of redoubling his efforts to find work, he reportedly cheered himself up by partying, drinking, and spending stacks of Leeza's money. (Or maybe he just didn't like staying at home and watching *Entertainment Tonight*. The English are accustomed to serious star-trashing in the press, not puffery.)

Leeza couldn't relate to that kind of defeatism. She's ambitious and a workaholic, and would never have let the system beat her. More important, that wasn't the kind of home environment she wanted for herself or newborn son Alexi, who was conceived on their honeymoon.

Unlike Valerie Bertinelli or Susan Linville, fast-track Leeza bailed out at the first sign of trouble. She filed for divorce on February 5 and, shortly thereafter, Chris returned to England. No time for backstabbing or pettiness. In a perverse way, one has to admire that kind of assertiveness.

Relationships can be tough to maintain anywhere, but TV adds special pressures: sudden wealth and fame that warp one's values; the opposite, constant rejection or failure in front of millions of viewers and snide critics; emotional and sometimes physical intimacy with fellow actors week after week; long hours away from home; and golddiggers and opportunists who seduce or fawn on stars. Almost no one is immune: even that epitome of family men, long-married Bill Cosby, has been linked in the tabloids to at least two women in recent years—a young blackjack dealer in Las Vegas, and a schoolteacher.

Maybe the solution is that marriages in TV Babylon

should be contracted-for like series: thirteen weeks with an option to renew, custody of the spin-offs to be determined.

Coldblooded and tacky? Yes.

And perfect for TV Babylon.

Battle of the Network Stars

Costarring situations are very much like marriages: you're with a person day after day, for long hours, and while there are many pleasant and rewarding times, there are also disagreements. Unlike marriages, however, actors don't choose their costars. Nor is there a period of "living together," to make sure the people are compatible. The casting choices are made, and everyone hopes for the best.

The arguments that arise between actors might be about how to play a scene or who should be the focus of the action. Never mind that questions like these *should* be decided by the director: in TV Babylon, it's the stars who carry the weight.

Battles between stars and directors or between stars and producers (almost always over money) invariably don't last long because the star is the draw and is usually mollified with more money or the dismissal of the offending person or persons. Once in a rare while, if there's a strong ensemble cast, producers will take a chance and give the star the boot. That's what happened with Valerie Harper of NBC's *Valerie*. There are few TV actresses who are kinder and more cooperative than Valerie. Even considerate stars can have salary disputes, however, and, when one arose, Valerie was fired. The show continued as *Valerie's Family* (later, *The Hogan Family*) with Sandy Duncan in the lead, and it remained a hit. (Not that NBC came out on top. Feeling that an agreement *had* been reached, and that she'd been unfairly and punitively dismissed, Valerie sued the production company and won $1.85 million.)

However, when there are two stars of equal weight spatting with each other—just as in a troubled marriage—the results can be fireworks.

Some of the tensions that have enveloped soundstages in recent years are more like a few Roman candles than a full-out Fourth of July display. When he became the heartthrob hit of *The Hogan Family* (which is why Valerie was no longer deemed essential), Jason Bateman reportedly started throwing his weight around. Tony Danza allegedly feuded with Alyssa Milano and Judith Light, his costars on *Who's the Boss*, over whose character should have more airtime. Mary Frann and Bob Newhart were said to be at odds over the dowdy approach to her character (she didn't like it). Pick a show, and there have been reports of dissent.

Most actors want to preserve their big-bucks salaries, however, and few tiffs have ever gotten completely out of control. As discussed elsewhere in this book, *Roseanne* came close. But the champion disaster area of all time is *Moonlighting*, the hit series that self-destructed.

Valerie Harper at an impromptu press conference after winning her suit against Lorimar/Telepictures for $1.85 million. (AP/Wide World)

Moonlighting premiered in 1985. Superficially, it was a show about detective Maddie Hayes (Cybill Shepherd) and her lover/associate David Addison (Bruce Willis) of the Blue Moon Detective Agency in Los Angeles. The main appeal, however, was not the mysteries, but the show's hip unpredictability—one week it did *The Taming of the Shrew* in period costume, another week a spoof of *Casablanca*—and the interaction between the two stars.

But the stars were not happy with one another. For Shepherd, this was a comeback vehicle. She was thirty-six when the show debuted, and both her film and TV career were a disaster area. Her last series, *The Yellow Rose*, had died a quick death in 1983. Her TV films, from *A Guide for the Married Woman* (1978) to *Seduced* (1985), hadn't set the world on fire. She was a battered veteran who needed desperately for this show to succeed.

For the thirty-year-old Willis, *Moonlighting* was his first shot at series TV. A New York stage actor and former bartender, he'd started working in TV only a few years before, guest-starring in *Miami Vice*, *Hart to Hart*, and other series before landing the role of Addison.

At first, both stars were glad to have the work. Even though the scripts were constantly late, and it was often necessary to work fourteen hours a day, everyone felt that they were putting together a quality show. And they were. *Moonlighting* debuted and shot to the top of the ratings. When it did, however, things changed. Cybill had been here before, so ego wasn't a problem with her . . . even though she was *extremely* concerned about how she looked and how she was photographed, which occasionally held up production.

But Bruce was worse: he got cocky. He landed a multimillion-dollar endorsement contract with Seagram, pushing their product in TV ads. He was offered movie deals. And there were women. As former girlfriend Sheri Rivera (ex-wife of Geraldo) put it, Willis could not help "eyeballing everything in skirts or tight pants." They did more than eyeball the hot star back.

Cybill says, "Bruce went from being an unknown and having no money to being enormously wealthy, having access to drugs and alcohol, having power. That's very difficult to deal with."

Bruce dealt with it by partying, though his exploits didn't make news in 1987. Neighbors complained about the loud music he was playing at his home, and he refused to turn it down. The police was called and, when they showed up at his door, Willis grew indignant. Not only wouldn't he turn down the music, he began shoving the police and swearing. He was rewarded with a trip to the slammer, where he spent several hours. But the worst was yet to come: Seagram apparently decided that a guy who pushes law officers shouldn't push their wine coolers, and that was the end of Willis's endorsement deal (the company tried to put a face-saving spin on it, maintaining that the successful promotion had run its natural course).

The incident seemed to make Willis rebellious rather than repentant. He began showing up drunk on the set, and although Cybill found that objectionable, she didn't resent it nearly as much as when he began demanding changes in his character—changes that affected the way her own part was written.

At first, Willis's Addison was extremely likable but not too bright, whereas Maddie was smart but a little

chilly. The actor wanted that changed. He insisted that
Addison be likable *and* smart. Because Willis was
pulling in female viewers, the audience advertisers
most want to reach, the producers obliged—but in
order to do that, they had to make Maddie less clever
at times, so the characters would continue to create
sparks.

This didn't sit well with Cybill, and, during rehears-
als, discussions about the dialogue evolved into arguments that blossomed into full-scale battles. Like a
flood, these regularly spilled from the set to someone's
trailer to the production offices. Cybill recalls that
they "would sometimes scream at each other for thirty
minutes or so."

At the time, Cybill *swore* the fights weren't as vitri-
olic as they sounded. "With Bruce and me . . . we're
more like kids fighting. When you're working with
someone for nine or ten months straight, you go
through periods when you hate each other's guts."
But, she said, it wasn't antagonism. "It's more like
competition. When I look back on what we've done
together, I'm so impressed. He's so talented, so really
talented."

Willis agreed. "I mean, who doesn't compete," he
said. "I think the most accurate description is that it's
playful one-upmanship."

But "really talented" or not, Bruce began meddling
in other areas that really ticked Cybill off. One of the
greatest fights they had was over the way Maddie wore
her hair. Cybill chose to give her character "an
uptight, traditional hairstyle." Willis never thought
that was right, and finally said so. He felt that Maddie
should have a sexier look. He was also fed up with
how long it took Cybill to do her hair, and Cybill says

that when he bugged her "one time too many" about that, she shot back at the balding costar, "Well, at least I *have* some!"

All that accomplished was to make Willis preen even longer before the cameras rolled. Sometimes, he didn't let the hairdresser start working on his hair until Cybill was on the set and waiting. Naturally, her hair wilted under the lights and, by the time Willis arrived, she'd need to have her hair retouched.

Because of the problems with the stars and the challenge of coming up with innovative episodes each week, *Moonlighting* fell way behind schedule. Reruns were constantly being aired and, over two seasons, the show's following eroded. That caused even greater tension on the set, with each star blaming the other for the delays. Moreover, Willis was frustrated by a film career that suddenly seemed to stall due to the back-to-back flops of *Blind Date* (1986) and *Sunset* (1988).

Then Cybill got pregnant. Nothing wrong with that, except that stories had to be written to explain *how* the single Maddie got that way. That made for long delays and unhappiness on Bruce's part. He refused, for example, to let the writers marry Addison and Maddie, feeling that would destroy the relationship by removing its parrying, flirtatious qualities.

Meanwhile, because Cybill was often sick and uncomfortable, production was held up even further. There was also rumors of trouble in her marriage to chiropractor Bruce Oppenheim (the two eventually divorced), which didn't improve her disposition. By the end of the third season, Cybill says she was so "upset I just couldn't function." However, there was hope on the horizon.

Willis had met and fallen in love with actress Demi
Moore. A health fanatic, she got Bruce to go to Alcoholics Anonymous, and that made a big difference in
his personality. Bruce said at the time that with Demi
and sobriety, "I feel balanced and very centered."
Cybill concurs. She says that when he showed up
sober for what was to be the last season of *Moonlighting*, not only was life on the set "easier," but she
was "really proud of him."

Ironically, by the time a semblance of peace had
been restored to the set, the ratings had fallen so
low—due to constant reruns—that *Moonlighting* was
canceled. Since then, Bruce's career has soared with
commercial hits like *Die Hard* (1988) and *Die Hard
II (1990), and critical successes like In Country* (1989).
Cybill made one terrible film, *Texasville* (1990), and
nothing else—but she will undoubtedly make another
comeback in a suitable TV vehicle.

Anyone who survived *Moonlighting* is not about to
be stopped by a bad film or two.

Out Foxx and Other Tales
from the Poorhouse

Bankruptcy.

Among the rich and powerful in TV Babylon, it may be the dirtiest of all words. Worse than alcoholism and far worse than divorce. For once you file those papers, not only are your finances made public, but you're admitting to the industry and to the audience that you're no longer hot. Among the superficial denziens of TV Babylon, that perception is the kiss of death. No one wants to be associated with a loser, and even if you *do* get work, producers know they can hire you cheap. The projects you'll be offered are usually subpar, with the result that you'll slide further into oblivion.

Ironically, it isn't always a sign of irresponsibility when a person goes bust. Because image is so important, the facade of wealth must be kept up. It's the price of doing business in Hollywood, and borderline or former stars hope that the work comes in before the money runs out. For instance—

There was a time when Cheryl Stoppelmoor looked like a sure bet for TV superstardom. She came to Los Angeles from South Dakota as a singer with a small band, began doing voices for cartoon characters, and, propelled by her wholesome beauty, quickly made her way into prime-time TV as a regular on *The Ken Berry "Wow" Show* in 1972. Five years later, at the age of twenty-six, she was named to replace Farrah Fawcett as one of *Charlie's Angles*. Married to actor David Ladd, son of movie legend Alan Ladd, Cheryl Ladd seemed to have it all.

When *Charlie's Angeles* ended in 1981, Cheryl began doing TV movies, the highest profile one of which was *Grace Kelly* in 1983. She also got herself a new husband, David's good friend, producer Brian Russell (a union covered in our previous volume).

Unfortunately, competition for parts is fierce in the "aging beauty" bracket. Former "Angels" Farrah Fawcett and Jacqueline Smith made the transition to serious dramatic roles and miniseries, respectively, but they're the exceptions.

Work dried up for Cheryl, but the expenses did not: there was the $3.4-million home in the Hollywood Hills (monthly mortgage payment: more than $7,000, plus another $3,500 for maintenance), the mortgage on a second home (monthly payment: $1,300), and other expenses ranging from child support and tuition ($1,300) to legal fees ($5,000 monthly) to recreation ($5,850 a month).

In 1989, between the two of them, the Russells earned slightly over $40,000 a month, while their expenses were nearly $62,000. Next stop: bankruptcy court. In February of 1990, the couple filed for Chapter Eleven protection from their creditors.

It was distressing to see the once-bright star fall on hard times; hopefully, she'll recover. Conversely, only a saint could hurt for the abrasive and inflammatory Morton Downey, Jr., whose fortunes took a downturn when his syndicated hate-fest, *The Morton Downey, Jr. Show,* was canned in 1989 after a two-year run. He was fifty-six at the time, and though he'd tried to branch out into writing (with a flop autobiography; his audience doesn't—can't?—read) and recording (he cut—or rather, slashed—an album of songs), Downey had failed, abysmally. Maybe he should have tried cigarette endorsements.

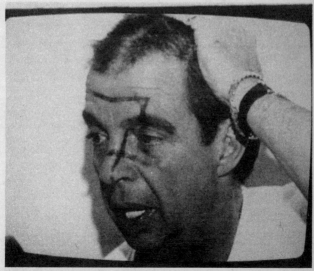

Victim or buffoon? Morton Downey, Jr., tells a TV interviewer how three youths attacked him in the lavatory of San Francisco International Airport, cutting his hair and painting a swastika on his face. (AP/Wide World)

On April 24, 1989, he made what many assumed to
be a pitiful stab for publicity by claiming that he was
attacked by skinheads in an airport restroom, the neo-
Nazis cutting his hair and drawing a swastika on his
face. The "damage" was widely presumed to have
been self-inflicted, and instead of inspiring outrage
merely made Downey seem like a pathetic figure.
That impression reinforced when he subsequently filed
for bankruptcy, listing his assets as $320 in the bank
and $100 in his pocket. Total liabilities: $2.4 million,
including a $628,000 mortgage and a half-million-dol-
lar federal tax bill.

Downey has since made halting returns to the public
eye, staring in an episode of the HBO series *Tales
from the Crypt* (playing—what else?—an obnoxious
TV host), and appearing as a heckler in a segment of
the cable comedy showcase *Caroline's Comedy Hour.*

It's not pretty, but Downey's clawing his way back.
Whether he deserves to or not, he'll probably make
it.

Easily the most disturbing financial crash of them
all was the one suffered by comedian Redd Foxx, who
had *really* paid his show business dues and seemed to
deserve some measure of security. But, foolishly, he
was negligent with the IRS, and for a while it was
open season for Foxx hunters.

A nightclub comic and recording artist noted for
his extremely blue albums, Foxx began making guest
appearances on TV in the early sixties, showing up on
series like *Mr. Ed*, *Green Acres*, and *The Addams
Family.* In 1972, he was cast as grouchy junkman Fred
Sanford on *Sanford and Son*, which ran for five seasons. He followed this with *Redd Foxx* in 1977 and

Sanford in 1980, both of which failed to equal the success of the comedian's first series.

Notwithstanding the subsequent failures, Foxx had gotten accustomed to living well on the $4 million a year he'd earned during his *Sanford and Son* days. And although good living is no crime, Foxx neglected to pay his taxes, which is. In 1983, with assets of $2.1 million, but owing $1.6 to the IRS and $800,000 to other creditors, he filed for Chapter Eleven bankruptcy. The court ordered Foxx to sell various properties he owned in southern California to pay the debt, and that was done. The comedian didn't pay everything he owed, however, nor did he pay all his taxes in 1983, 1984, and 1986. Thus, by the end of 1989, with penalties and interest added, his bill totaled $1,753,344.50—not counting additional taxes he owed to both California and New Jersey, which brought the total to $2.9 million.

In fairness to the IRS, Foxx was making little more than a halfhearted effort to pay the bills. He'd recently been paid a half million dollars to appear in the Eddie Murphy film *Harlem Nights*, and, according to the IRS, spent $373,000 of that on "wine, women, song and gambling." Only in August, with the specter of a raid looming over him, did Foxx begin making some serious payments, turning over most of the $20,000 he was earning each week from his shows at the Hacienda Hotel. However, it was too little, too late.

Shortly after dawn on November 28, seventeen armed agents swooped down on the Las Vegas home of the sixty-six-year-old Foxx. They took eight cars, $13,000 in cash, a dozen guns, every scrap of furniture except the bed, and all of his jewelry—including the rings he was wearing, and a watch that had been given

Redd Foxx in an episode of *Sanford and Son*. Little did the comedian know that one day, life would imitate art. (AP/ Wide World)

to him by Elvis Presley. They even confiscated the doghouse of his Great Dane, Groucho. As for the house itself, the agents said the comedian could remain there until it was sold. Foxx was so over-wrought by the raid that a doctor was called to come and sedate him.

The IRS planned to auction the 400 separate items. However, Foxx's attorney was able to convince the bankruptcy court to grant a sixty-day stay so they could try and work things out. The deal they hammered out was that the cars and jewelry would be auctioned to reduce Foxx's debt, his other possessions would be returned, and Foxx would be more diligent about paying the back taxes as well as current and future bills. Shortly thereafter, to help meet this goal, Foxx opened a store in Las Vegas called Fred G. Sanford, in which he sold his own possessions as well as mementos from his TV shows.

Though Foxx had dug his own hole, it was easy to feel sorry for the comedian: until he finally clicked on national TV, he hadn't had an easy life. All things considered, though, he got off lucky. To paraphrase Fred Sanford, "Elizabeth—I dodged the big one!"

Living it Up, Living it Down

It's virtually impossible for anyone in TV Babylon—
or in movies, politics, or business, for that matter—to
have a shady past and *not* have it discovered. There's
always an old "friend" willing to sell reminiscences, a
photographer happy to peddle a compromising photo-
graph, that old porn film an actor made when starva-
tion loomed, or court records that are open to the
public.

Sometimes, the news is barely shocking. When
America's Favorite Home Videos became the hottest
show of 1989, TV fans who browsed through the comedy racks at local videotape stores learned that host
Bob Saget isn't as wholesome as he appears. He's a
costar of two stand-up comedy cassettes: *Your Favorite Laughs From An Evening At the Improv* and *Paramount Comedy Theater, Volume One: Well-Developed*.
In these, Saget swears and tells jokes about masturba-
tion, sex, drugs, homosexuality, and various other R-
rated topics. Fans who only know Saget from *Ameri-*

ca's Favorite Home Videos or his sitcom *Full House* would be horrified to see the act that first got him national attention in the early 1980s.

But in a world where raw comedians like Eddie Murphy or Andrew Dice Clay can be toned down, marketed, and thrust into the mainstream, Saget's situation is hardly unique.

Sometimes it isn't the star who's got a past, but someone with whom they're associated. In that respect, Rue McClanahan of *Golden Girls* rates high on the sucker scale. For more than a year, the fifty-six-year-old actress dated sixty-year-old Dirk Summers, whom she'd met at a rally for animal rights, even though she knew nothing about his background. Turns out that in December of 1987, the balding, bespectacled Summers had been sentenced to three years, eight months in prison for felony theft and fraud. He was released on parole after a year. Prior to that, he'd been accused of numerous other crimes, from reportedly having forged Liberace's signature on a letter endorsing a celebrity golf tournament to allegedly trying to have a former business partner knocked off.

Rue knew none of this. She was blinded by infatuation, and when her costars tried to tell her that the man was a smooth, sweet-talking fake, she refused to listen. Finally, in April of 1990, the tabloids began printing details of his exploits, and Summers confessed, in a wonderful understatement, "I haven't told her everything—there isn't time for everything."

Rue, who has been married six times, obviously marches to her own drummer when it comes to romance. However, she got the message about Dirk; they split, and she began dating twenty-nine-year-old marketing executive Michael Thornton . . . who is three years younger than Rue's son!

It's slightly more surprising when someone who's become one of America's sweethearts proves to have a shady past. When Mel Harris (Yuppie supermom Hope of *thirtysomething*) was twenty-one years old and a model, she was dragged into a murder trial in 1980: seems the body of a drug dealer was found in a gun crate owned by Mel's fiancé, David Silbergeld. The boyfriend of one of Mel's girlfriends was found guilty of the crime and sent to prison. As for Mel, she married Silbergeld; they were divorced before their first anniversary.

(Mel also committed a bit of fraud of her own: although she says she was married only once before tying the knot with *Equal Justice* star Cotter Smith in November of 1988, she'd been married to Silbergeld, to Manhattanite Brian Kilclinic, and to Pulitzer Prize-winning photographer David Hume Kennerly. She divorced Kennerly six months before marrying Smith. Sounds more like *three*something, eh Mel?)

Even seamier than Mel's background, though, was that of *Wheel of Fortune* hostess Vanna White. Prior to landing the show in 1983, Vanna had had an unspectacular acting career, appearing in a handful of theatrical films such as *Looker* (1981) and *Graduation Day* (1981), and in the TV movie *Midnight Offering* (1981), about teenage witches. That year, she was also the star of a film, *Gypsy Angels*, in which she did a topless sex scene. The film ran into legal troubles and was shelved *until* Vanna became famous—*then* it was completed and released.

Before all of this activity, though, the only career Vanna had was as a kept woman.

In 1979, the twenty-two-year-old South Carolina native moved from Atlanta—where she'd had modest success as a model—to Las Vegas, where she hoped to start a career in show business.

Introduced to a popular Vegas singer through a mutual friend, Paula (not her real name), Vanna became the married singer's mistress. She spent most of her time at a Los Angeles apartment for which he footed the bill, and also took acting lessons for which he also paid. Occasionally she traveled to be with him—when the singer wasn't with his wife or other two ladyfriends.

At the time, Vanna weighed 145 pounds, which gave her a well-rounded Gina Lollobrigida look. She wasn't happy with that and decided to diet away some forty pounds. But that was easier said than done and, as Paula says, "Using cocaine also helped her lose weight. I saw her high on cocaine a number of times. I also saw her smoking pot several times." When she reached her present weight of 108, Vanna cut back on substance abuse.

The relationship with the singer lasted six months, ending when he tried to reach Vanna at her apartment in Los Angeles one weekend and couldn't. He thought she was out with another man; in fact, she was out with Paula, at Disneyland. The singer ended the relationship at once.

According to Paula, Vanna was so upset that "she threw herself into a nonstop round of parties and men," including a brief friendship with *Playboy* publisher Hugh Hefner. She spent a great deal of time at the Playboy Mansion in southern California, lounging around topless in the sun. More and more, she spent time there with soap opera star John Gibson, who

Vanna White and a dapper Sylvester Stallone. Years before, her "dates" were of a somewhat different nature. (UPI/Bettmann)

became her lover; tragically, he was killed on May 17, 1986, in a plane crash. After that, Vanna could no longer bear going to the mansion with its memories. The film and TV roles followed, after which she won the part of letter-turner on *Wheel of Fortune*. Ironically, she had a falling out with her old friend Hef when the ailing *Playboy* printed seminude lingerie shots she'd allowed to have taken in 1982. Sales for that issue were extraordinary.

Incidentally, although Vanna has earned fame and fortune from the show, she's very disappointed at being known as a one-trick pony. Alas, if the horseshoe fits. . . . A commercially disastrous, far-from-candid autobiography was an embarrassment, and her acting career stalled after she starred in the highly touted, go-nowhere TV movie *Goddess of Love* (1988), in which she played the Roman deity Venus, and guest appearances on *L.A. Law* in the fall of 1990, in which she played herself. Her career setbacks were put on the back burner on New Year's Eve 1990, however, as she wed longtime boyfriend George Santo Pietro, a Los Angeles restaurateur.

Vanna's past (and probably future) is not dissimilar from that of many attractive young women (and young men, for that matter) who come to TV Babylon with big dreams. As it happens, compared to the past of another of TV's sweethearts, Vanna was an angel.

Since October of 1986, Susan Ruttan has played law-office secretary Roxanne Melman on the phenomenally successful prime-time series *L.A. Law*. Roxanne is a soft-spoken, maternal woman who has had little success in romance, and is not-so-secretly in love with her boss, swinging divorce attorney Arnie Becker (played by Corbin Bernsen).

In real life, the much-adored Susan Ruttan is almost as demure as Roxanne—despite her $300,000-a-year salary. Her one obvious extravagance is a BMW convertible; otherwise, she's a down-to-earth woman who keeps to herself and doesn't like to attract attention. But that's the Susan of today. According to her ex-sister-in-law, Frances Pollin, the Susan *she* knew "was a druggie and a devious, sneaky bitch."

Born Susan Dunrud in 1949, in Oregon City, Oregon, the future actress had an unhappy childhood and ran away from home when she was still in her early teens. She eventually ended up in juvenile court and, as a result, Susan was sent to the Convent of the Good Shepherd in Portland, a school for wayward girls. Moving to Santa Rosa, California, upon graduation in 1967, she hung out with bikers—which is how she met her future husband, handsome, intense-looking Mel Ruttan. A decorated Vietnam veteran, the career soldier was out with a buddy when he saw Susan at a biker's hangout. She was wearing a miniskirt (no underwear) and high heels; she was also extremely dirty.

Mel went over to the young girl. He felt sorry for her and convinced her to come to his mother's house to clean up. Susan ended up staying there, Mel offering to help her get a job and to pay for training so she could do something useful with her life. She decided to become a nurse.

They were married six months later, in August of 1967, but the marriage didn't start off auspiciously. Both of the Ruttans did drugs—pot, LSD, and downers—and Susan really had no desire to be a nurse *or* a homemaker. She let the house go to seed while she spent her free time buying clothes (she managed to run up a tab of $5,000 at one store) or meeting with her old biker buddies, and in many cases sleeping with them.

Though Mel didn't know about the affairs, he was disgusted with the clothes bills and with Susan's unproductive lifestyle. They fought frequently and, exactly two years after they married, Mel filed for divorce. Shortly thereafter, he returned to Vietnam; while he was gone, Frances says Susan "partied constantly with drugs and men."

Wounded in action, Mel was sent back to the United States to recuperate, after which he was stationed in Germany. Susan remained in the States until her money ran out, then, in July of 1970, contacted Mel in Germany, suggesting a reconciliation. She seemed sincere, and he was amenable, so Susan flew over. Unfortunately, the two continued to fight and, by the end of October, when Mel returned to the United States, he decided to go through with the divorce. The papers were completed and in Mel's hands by the end of November.

Mel's mother Frances says, "He was delighted" when he got the decree, and got onto his motorcycle to show it to Susan. Tragically, his bike skidded into a telephone pole and he died.

Susan did not attend the funeral, nor did she phone his family. For that, the Ruttans could probably have forgotten Susan and gotten on with their lives. However, the young woman did something which they considered despicable: she retained an attorney to try and get the divorce annulled, so that she could collect on Mel's $10,000 insurance policy. The case went to trial and, while on the stand, Susan confessed that during the marriage she'd used drugs and slept with other men. She could hardly deny it: a trio of photographs was introduced as evidence, all of them showing Susan in the buff with two other men. Susan also admitted that she hadn't bothered to claim her husband's body.

Yet—the worst of these infractions had taken place before Susan's trip to Germany. The courts considered her efforts at reconciliation to have been sincere, and the divorce was voided. Susan collected the money; the Ruttans were horrified.

"Susan Ruttan destroyed my family," Frances says today. Understandably, Susan herself takes a slightly different view. She doesn't deny any of what happened (indeed, in 1973, she hired a lawyer to retrieve those revealing photos from court records), but says of the Ruttans, "I feel sad for them. A lot of people have done a lot of growing up since then."

Susan *has* changed. She became an actress to earn a living, and has turned her life around, just as Vanna turned her life around. TV audiences may be shocked to learn about shady pasts, but they usually like a celebrity well enough to forgive a wayward lifestyle that's been put behind them.

Celebrities who complain about the burdens of fame would do well to remember that; try to imagine a politician or CEO of a major corporation being allowed to get on with their career if any *one* of these things were discovered in their past!

Family Ties

It's often a surprise when we turn on the tube or open a magazine and encounter the relatives of the rich and famous. Rarely, if ever, do they have the magnetism or charm of their famous sibling, offspring, nephew, or niece. If they *did*, then, obviously, the world would be full of TV stars!

Sometimes, though, there *are* formidable personalities in a star's past, people who have left scars of one kind or another.

Lucie Arnaz has said of mother Lucille Ball, "She was a control freak. She had to be in charge twenty-four hours a day." However, Lucie wasn't traumatized by her mother. She argued with her, and she moved out when they could no longer get along—but that wasn't much different from what many teenagers go through. Carol Burnett's parents were both alcoholics who died from alcohol-related diseases at the age of forty-six. But they never abused her—only themselves—and she has always been able to focus on the

good times they had when her folks were sober.
Unhappily, alocholism, too, is quite common.

The experiences of Woody Harrelson and Dirk Benedict are different from what most people go through.
Incredibly so.

Since 1985, Woody Harrelson has starred as Woody
Boyd, the goofy bartender on *Cheers*. You wouldn't
think it to talk to the good-natured actor, but he's got
a wicked lineage: Woody Harrelson is the son of a
hit man. According to the extraordinary book *High
Treason*, he may also have played a role in the assassination of President John Kennedy.

In 1973, Charles Harrelson was paid handsomely to
pump several bullets into the back of the head of
Texas businessman Sam Degelia, Jr. Six years later,
he was given a quarter of a million dollars to eliminate
a higher-profile target: Federal Judge "Maximum"
John Wood, whom a powerful drug dealer wanted out
of the way.

Hiding outside Wood's home in San Antonio, Harrelson assassinated him with one bullet from a high-
powered rifle. Captured, tried, and found guilty, the
killer is presently serving a twenty-year sentence for
firearms and cocaine convictions, after which he'll
start his life sentence for the murder of Judge Wood.

When Charles was arrested, his ex-wife took their
sons Woody and younger brother Brett from Texas to
Ohio. They never knew what their father had done;
all their mother told them, Brett says, is that their
father "lived and worked in Texas." It wasn't until
Woody was fourteen that his mother told the boys the
truth. Both took it hard and, understandably, have
wanted to see their father retried. As Brett points out,

"I know he didn't receive a fair trial. He was tried in a courthouse named after the dead judge."

It's impossible to say how much Woody was affected by these events. It would be fair to say, however, that he has more than the average person's angst about his paternal roots.

Traumatic as that revelation was to the Harrelson boys, it pales beside the fatherly grief suffered by a youthful Dirk Benedict, star of *Chopper One* (1974), *Battlestar Galactica* (1978), and *The A-Team* (1983–1987).

In 1963, Benedict, then nineteen, lived in a small house in White Sulphur Springs, Montana, with his older brother Roy, twenty-two, younger sister Ramona, and mother Priscilla. Priscilla was divorced from Dirk's father, lawyer George E. Niewoehner, who was under a court order to stay away from the woman. Though George was a loving father—especially with young Dirk, his fishing and tennis companion—he had a nasty temper, and Priscilla was afraid of what he might do to her. Even two years after the divorce, a psychiatrist had described George as "dangerous."

He was right.

On August 4, 1963, a Sunday morning, the fifty-one-year-old man defied the court order and went to see his former wife. He entered her downstairs bedroom and, not surprisingly, an argument erupted. Priscilla told him that she didn't want him there to see his kids or whatever else he had in mind; instead of leaving, however, George began beating Priscilla.

Her cries awakened Roy, who bolted from bed. Not sure what he'd find downstairs, he grabbed his hunting rifle and ran from his room. When the young man saw his father punching his mother, blood on her face and

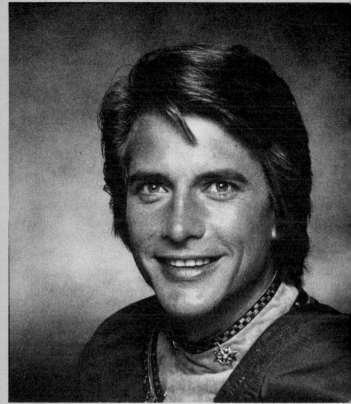

Dirk Benedict on *Battlestar Galactica*. (© ABC-TV)

on his hands, he shouted at his father to leave. But either the man didn't hear or wasn't listening, and he continued to hit Priscilla.

Fearing that the man was going to kill her—if not now, then some other time—Roy raised the rifle, aimed, and put a bullet in his father's chest. George gasped and staggered back several steps, then collapsed on the floor. Roy ran to Priscilla.

Upon hearing the shot, Dirk came downstairs to find his brother holding their mother, who was shrieking, their father sprawled on the floor beside her. Blood was everywhere. Screaming, Dirk turned and ran out the back door and pounded his fists on an outside wall until they were raw. Then he ran to the driveway and locked himself in the car, crying hysterically.

When police arrived, Dirk could barely speak to them. He was sent to stay with a friend, where, for eight hours straight, he sat at the piano and played mournful songs. As for Roy, the shooting was declared "justifiable homicide to prevent his mother's death and to protect his own life," and Roy was set free.

Although TV Babylon didn't cause any of these tragedies, it's touched by them through the work of the actors. Whatever qualities other performers might bring to their roles, Harrelson and Benedict bring what the latter once described as "a real desire to help viewers forget, for as long as they're with us, some of their own problems. That's my job."

One thing Benedict neglected to mention: it's very much, too, their own means of escape.

Raging Rivers

"I was the ugliest child ever born in Larchmont, New York," Joan Rivers once joked. "The doctor looked at me and slapped my mother."

It wasn't that bad, of course. For a time, however, it seemed like Joan, if not the ugliest child ever born in Larchmont, was certainly one of the unluckiest.

Born in 1933, the "Can we talk?" comedienne began her career at the age of twenty-five, when she left her husband and her job as a fashion coordinator to work as a gag writer and stand-up comedienne. She appeared at every spot that would have her ("If a trash can had a bulb, I played it") before being spotted at one of these "dumps" by a talent scout for *The Tonight Show*. She made her debut there in 1965 and was a smash. Thereafter, Joan appeared regularly on the show, between engagements in Las Vegas and high-class theaters around the nation. She was named the show's official guest host in 1983, appearing whenever Johnny Carson was on vacation.

Somehow, Joan found time to get married for a second time, to Edgar Rosenberg, and have a daughter, Melissa, born in 1968.

Rivers was popular and controversial: her jokes about sex, marriage, and even Elizabeth Taylor's weight gain ("She's the only woman I know who stands in front of the microwave yelling, 'Faster!' ") were widely deemed to have crossed the boundary of good taste, and her raucus, seallike laugh grated on many peoples' nerves. But she tapped into the frustrations and concerns of many women, and her following was large and devoted.

Yet, Joan wasn't satisfied. She was frustrated by the prospect of living in Carson's shadow forever, and by persistent rumors that the network was looking for someone hipper and male to replace her. Thus, in 1986, Rivers jumped at the opportunity to host her own talk show on the brand new Fox network—*The Late Show Starring Joan Rivers*.

Unfortunately, she hadn't discussed the matter with Johnny, and word of the deal reached the press before she could phone him. When she finally got around to calling, Carson refused to talk to her. Frankly, it's tough to blame him: he was her mentor, and now she was going against him. The least she could have done was discuss the offer with him before agreeing to jump ship. And while Joan would obviously have preferred to retain Johnny's friendship, the rift garnered wide publicity, which certainly didn't hurt Joan's cause.

The show debuted on October 9, 1986, and, after some promising ratings initially, it sunk fast. Fearful of being unofficially blacklisted from Carson's show, many top stars refused to appear with Joan. Moreover, she had toned down her style considerably: she

Joan Rivers with, from the left, Melissa, Edgar, announcer Clint Holmes, and musical director Mark Hudson. The cake was a surprise from the cast and crew after Joan taped her last *Late Show*. The cake reads, WE LOVE JOAN! YOUR FRIENDS ON THE STAFF AND CREW. (UPI/Bettmann)

was uncharacteristically fawning to the stars who did appear. It was painful to see the once-brash cat become a kitten.

By March, the show had less than half the audience it had had in October. Joan was growing frazzled, and behind the scenes the show was a nightmare. Edgar was co-executive producer, and had had a lot of input into the show, originally. As it began to falter after the first few weeks, Joan said, "He can't sleep. He has to take sleeping pills. He thinks about the show all night long. After the show we talk about it. In the morning we talk about it. It's constant. And he keeps battling for me. He's like the only one almost on my side."

In April, Fox made things easier for Edgar. Feeling that Joan was too protective of Edgar, and Edgar of Joan—to the detriment of the finished product—network president Jamie Kellner told Edgar that he was no longer to come to the set or be involved in the show's day-to-day decision making.

In essence, Edgar was fired.

Joan was crushed. Her on-air performance became lackluster, and she didn't last much longer, departing after the May 15 broadcast. Ironically, she was replaced by hip, male Arsenio Hall, and the show made him a star.

Joan was relieved to be out of the maelstrom, but the story didn't end there. She was extremely depressed by her very visible failure, and Edgar blamed himself—as Joan's manager and producer—for many of the problems she'd had. But Edgar's problems were more than just emotional. Physically, he hadn't been well for quite some time. He'd given up a five-pack-a-day cigarette habit in 1984 after suffering a massive heart attack and undergoing quadruple bypass surgery. He was also addicted to Valium, and was suffering from gout, a haitus hernia, high blood pressure, and a bleeding ulcer.

On August 11, Edgar went to Philadelphia to take care of some real estate business with his dearest friend, Tom Pileggi. Several days later, on the night

of August 14, alone in his suite at the Four Seasons
Hotel, he phoned daughter Melissa. "I've put everything in order for you," he said. "You must be an
adult. Things are going to be very difficult."

Melissa was confused and asked him what he was
talking about.

He didn't explain. Later, he called back, speaking
to both Joan and Melissa, telling them both that he
was going to be coming home soon. After hanging up,
he called his psychiatrist and made an appointment.
Then he placed one more call, asking for a car to meet
him at the Los Angeles airport. It was to take him
directly to Cedars-Sinai Medical Center.

At this point, Edgar was still planning to go home.
He had once told his wife, "Suicide is a permanent
solution to a temporary problem," and he wasn't seriously considering ending his life. But after thinking
about it during the next few hours, he concluded that
his physical and emotional ills were *not* temporary.
That being the case, like the Japanese, he saw "ritual-
istic" suicide as a means of regaining the honor he
had lost in *The Late Show* debacle. He also saw it as
a way of fully accepting the blame, exonerating Joan,
and enabling her to reestablish her career.

Edgar sat down and set out two large envelopes.
In one marked JOAN ROSENBERG, he placed papers
pertaining to the estate, bank account numbers and
locations, and keys. In another marked MELISSA
ROSENBERG, he placed his money clip, which had
belonged to his own mother. He also enclosed notes
in each, declaring his love for both his ladies, but
adding—in Joan's—that she was better off without
him.

Sealing the envelopes, Edgar got the small cassette

recorder he carried and taped heartfelt messages to Joan and Melissa. He set those aside, next to the envelopes. Then he lay on the bed and took an overdose of Valium, washing it down with alcohol.

The next morning, Edgar's business associates tried to reach him. When they repeatedly got no answer, they phoned the desk and hotel security was sent to the room. They entered and found Rosenberg on the floor, a deep gash on his head. Later, Detective Gerald Wartenby said that he'd probably fallen out of bed and hit his head on the dresser.

Probably. Or maybe he'd changed his mind and was trying to get to the bathroom.

In any case, it was Melissa who answered the early-morning phone call from Philadelphia. Sobbing when she heard the terrible news, she composed herself as best as she could, then went to tell her mother.

The comedienne didn't believe it at first. But when the truth sunk in, she took out her rage by running into the bathroom, opening the medicine chest, and smashing bottle after bottle on the tile floor—all the while screaming, "You son of a bitch! *You son of a bitch!*"

Joan later blamed herself for what had happened, saying, "I should have seen the signs—his suddenly putting all his affairs in tiptop order." But, she adds that she was so "terribly depressed" by the failure of the show to think clearly. After the funeral, she said that she felt as though "two thirds of my life were gone: my career and my husband." What saved her from cracking up was the other third of her life—her daughter.

To get away from the media attention and to try and heal their emotional wounds, Joan and Melissa

Melissa and Joan leaving the Wilshire Boulevard Synagogue after a memorial service for Edgar. (UPI/Bettmann)

took a cruise to Greece. "We talked, cried, laughed, and got over the shock," Joan said. She also realized something else. "I had led a tremendously sheltered life. Edgar did literally everything else for me—the bills, contracts. I didn't know where the outside light switches were to the house. I had to become a big girl and put my life back together again by myself."

After her return to L.A., Joan received a great deal of support from the group Surviving After Suicide, and she recovered—not quite as quickly as the maga-

zine *GQ* suggested (she sued the publication for inti-
mating that she was callous about her husband's
death), although she did go back to work within
weeks. She had to. "My house has been filled with
friends," she said at the time. "But it's after they've
gone that it all hits. At four in the morning. That's
when you grieve. That's when it's so hard.

"Work is my catharsis. If I could have worked the
night Edgar died, I would have. And he would have
been the only one who understood my need to do
that. Work is helping me to cope."

She signed onboard as one of the *Hollywood
Squares*, agreed to appear on Broadway in Neil
Simon's *Broadway Bound*, and also went to work as a
spokeswoman for the jeans manufacturer No Excuses
(replacing the infamous Donna Rice). She also hit the
comedy-club circuit, humbly getting back to her roots
to rediscover herself, and actually making jokes about
Edgar's death ("I couldn't even identify my husband's
body," she cracked. "I hadn't looked at it for years.").

Today, her comedy sharp but bittersweet, Joan has
her own popular syndicated talk show, *The Joan Rivers Show*—for which she won a hard-earned Emmy
in 1990—and is well on the road to emotional and
professional recovery.

Which isn't to say Joan's life has been stress-free.
In the May 21, 1990, edition of *USA Today*, cocky
Bryant Gumbel of *The Today Show* was asked how
he was getting along with weathercaster Willard Scott,
with whom he'd had a feud over the leaked memo
(more on which in the chapter "Here Today, Gone
Tomorrow"). Gumbel told a newspaper interviewer
that all was well and, to prove it, invited "anybody to
come and watch us on and off the set."

Joan took him up on his offer.

Three days later, she asked for people in her studio audience to volunteer to go over to the NBC studios. Her party consisted of four housewives who, accompanied by two of her assistants, rode over to New York's Rockefeller Center where *The Today Show* is taped. They boarded an elevator, got off on the third floor— and were stopped by a guard. Words were exchanged and, when denied permission to see Gumbel, one of the visitors got so angry she struck a guard. Police were summoned, and by the time it was over, two women and both aides had been arrested. The other two women left and returned to Joan's studio at CBS, where the whole sorry saga was recounted on the air.

Joan was furious. "Those ladies are going to have to go to court and jail and God knows what. I don't think that's fair because Bryant extended an invitation." She added, "Bryant Gumbel owes me a public apology and flowers. And if I don't get them, I'll send myself flowers and charge them to him."

She never got the flowers, or an apology. Gumbel's a cur—but let's face it. Joan just doesn't get along with NBC hosts.

However, the women and her aides got off, and no real harm was done; this kind of controversy she can live with. More important, she managed to poke holes in a pompous figure *without* comedy. That helped to legitimize her as a serious talk-show host.

Today, Joan is remarkably together. She misses Edgar, of course, and still carries the pain of having lost the other man in her life, Johnny Carson. Not only haven't they spoken since 1986, but Johnny never even sent condolences upon Edgar's death. Nice guy.

Still, Joan will survive. She says that she's come through this with a brand new philosophy of life: "Enjoy the weekend and don't buy any green bananas."

And that's exactly what she's doing.

Soap Oprah

Fame is a two-edged sword. On the one hand, TV makes many of its stars and suppliers wealthy. But it robs them of their private life and, in many cases, exposes dark pasts and present-day secrets.

With the possible exception of Roseanne Barr, no one on TV has been as thoroughly studied, analyzed, and investigated as Oprah Winfrey. And like Roseanne, there are more than a few skeletons in the Winfrey closet.

To begin with, Oprah Gail Winfrey didn't have an auspicious debut. She was born out of wedlock; her father, Vernon, a soldier, was long gone by the time she came into the world on February 1, 1954. Not only that, but her mother Vernita had intended to call her the Biblical name Orpah, after Ruth's sister-in-law, but the midwife transposed the letters when she filled out the birth certificate.

Because her mother had to work, Oprah was raised by her grandmother on a pig farm outside of Kosciusko, Mississippi. By the age of six, the precocious girl had become too much for the old woman to handle and she was sent to Milwaukee to be with her mother, who earned her living doing housework. Too much of a handful for *her*, Oprah went to live in Nashville with her father, who was now a barber. But she missed her mother, and returned to Milwaukee a year after that.

Until she was nine, Oprah's life had been merely nomadic. After that, it became hell. When she was nine, she was raped by a nineteen-year-old cousin; during the next five years she was also sexually abused by other family "friends." She says, "I was always very needy, always in need of attention, and they just took advantage of that. There were people, certainly, around me who were aware of it, but they did nothing." Her younger siblings—half-brother Jeffrey and half-sister Patricia—were unaware of any problems; if they were around when one of Oprah's "guests" arrived, he would simply give them ice-cream pops and tell them to get lost.

Oprah became pregnant at the age of fourteen, and her mother sent her back to live with her father. She had the baby there, but the little boy was stillborn. Patricia said recently, "No one ever knew who was the father of Oprah's baby . . . it could have been any one of a lot of different guys." However, she says that "Oprah was devastated by her loss. She cried and cried. It broke her heart." Oprah herself says tersely, "The experience was the most emotional, confusing, and traumatic of my young life."

Oprah remained with her father and eventually won a scholarship to Tennessee State University. There, she became interested in broadcasting and broke into

A trimmed-down Oprah Winfrey in November of 1988.
Unfortunately, the great new look wouldn't last.
(AP/Wide World)

TV as an anchor at WTVF in Nashville. She switched to anchoring at WJZ-TV in Baltimore—where she suffered through an event that, her sister says, "hardened Oprah and drove her deeper and deeper into her career." The twenty-two-year-old met and fell in love with a married man. Although he loved her and wanted to continue seeing her, he wouldn't leave his wife. Oprah decided to go cold turkey on him, breaking off the relationship and throwing herself into work.

Oprah was invited to move to a bigger market, Chicago, where she began to attract serious attention with her morning show *People Are Talking*—not only because of her unique ability to become emotionally involved with her guests, but because when she went up against *Donahue*, she whipped him. If that wasn't gratifying enough, in 1984 she caught the eye of a Hollywood casting director and was offered a costarring role in the film *The Color Purple*. Oprah's performance won her an Oscar nomination and, in tandem with national syndication for her talk show, made her superrich and famous.

And happy?

TV makes many people wealthy, but it does so by making them public property. Oprah is worth more than a quarter of a *billion* dollars and lives both lavishly and generously, spending money on everything from a $50,000 Mercedes for her mother to hundreds of thousands of dollars to feed starving children worldwide. But her private life has had periods of disappointment and distress, exacerbated by the fact that she's so very much in the public eye.

For example, when she went on a 400-calorie-a-day diet and dropped from 190 to 123 pounds in just three months, the nation applauded. But when she put half of that back on again the following year, she had to endure very public censuring from women who regarded her as a role model, and from diet doctors who said she'd dropped the weight the wrong way to begin with. (She should have adopted more sensible eating habits and taken the weight off slowly, instead of crash-dieting. And she admits as much: "I ask God to keep mashed potatoes out of my life. I could go through my life and never eat a sweet thing. It's potatoes, pasta, bread, fried things." She adds that she has no intention of dieting again, and that fans and friends will have to accept her as is.

Oprah's name sells newspapers, and if she isn't dieting or gaining weight or discussing a teenage pregnancy, reporters will turn their pens on boyfriend Stedman Graham, a public relations executive, or other members of Oprah's family just to get her name in a headline. For instance—

At the same time that Oprah was being roasted for the weight gain, rumors began circulating about Graham, three years her senior and her boyfriend since 1986. There was talk that he was gay; one report even said that Oprah had knifed her beau after finding him in the arms of another man. Patricia recalls, "Oprah was absolutely furious (about the article)! She paced, she yelled, she hollered, she said, 'I can't believe people can be so cruel, spreading lies like that!' " There were also articles about her inability to hang on to this "neglected boyfriend" and their plans to marry— both in the same week!

Nor did the newsgathering efforts stop with Oprah's immediate circle. Jeffrey—who was gay—and Patricia both had grave problems, which made the papers. For years, Oprah supported Jeffrey . . . even though he had a nasty habit of blowing the money she gave him on cocaine. She forgave him repeatedly, and when he became ill with AIDS she paid his medical bills. Just before his death in December of 1989, the twenty-nine-year-old said, "Oprah disapproved of my life style and believes that homosexuality is wrong, but while hating the sin, she loves the sinner." Because of Oprah's fame, Jeffrey didn't die in peace; the tabloids covered his slow death in grim detail. (One interrupted an interview with the dying man to describe how, "His lips were covered with a white fungus.")

Similarly, thirty-one-year-old Patricia was using *her* monthly allowance of $1,200 from Oprah to buy cocaine. That, and Oprah's successful efforts to get her into rehabilitation, also captured a lot of ink.

Again—celebrities are fair game for the press. If the public wasn't intrigued by them, it wouldn't have made those people famous, and the loss of privacy is the price one pays for an eight-figure annual income. But the corollary is that being related to or close friends with a TV star is like hanging out with a mobster: if bullets start to fly, some of them may hit bystanders.

Midline Crisis

Oprah Winfrey is probably the most famous dieter this side of Elizabeth Taylor, but she's not the only one. Kirstie Alley of *Cheers* gained nearly thirty pounds after kicking cocaine and cigarettes. Susan Ruttan lost forty-five pounds and is now a svelte size eight. And while Sharon Gless was busy fighting a crazed fan, her former *Cagney and Lacey* costar Tyne Daly was unsuccessfully fighting the battle of the bulge, ballooning up during her starring stint in *Gypsy* on Broadway in 1989 to 1990.

Yet, the saddest saga of all is that of formerly-thin Delta Burke, the star of the CBS hit series *Designing Women*. A onetime beauty queen, she put on fifty pounds between the show's second and third seasons, the culmination of a series of emotionally wrenching events. Today, Delta talks openly about her many ordeals and, in a way, being heavy has liberated her. She no longer has to comport herself with a beauty queen's grace and style. "I can be myself," she says.

"I don't have to sit a certain way, or walk a certain way as I did in my glamour-puss days. I can be me."

But it was a tough haul achieving that kind of self-confidence. Very tough.

Professionally, the Orlando-born Delta has led a charmed life. Her climb to the top began in 1967, when she started modeling at the age of twelve. The winner of eighteen beauty pageants, including Miss Florida, she went to Hollywood in 1979, landed a part in the TV movie *Charleston*, and has been working ever since.

Delta Burke . . . starting on the road to a serious weight gain. (© Columbia Pictures Television)

Personally, though, her life has been one calamity after another. At the age of four, she was "touched and molested" by the father of a girlfriend, an incident that left her afraid that "every time a man approached me, he would hurt me. I sublimated that as best I could, but then as a teenager, I only met men who were interested in me sexually—and not romantically, but in a dirty, unloving way. I was nearly date-raped a number of times, and that pushed me over the edge. I became terrified of men."

When Delta came to Hollywood, not only didn't she date, she rarely left her apartment. Then, because of all the attention she received from *Designing Women*—especially from men—she says, "I turned to food for solace—like a baby sucking on a biscuit. I guess I also thought, subconciously, that if I were fat, men wouldn't find me attractive and I wouldn't have to deal with being a sex object.

"Actually," she says, "it wasn't as sudden as it seemed. I've always had trouble with my weight, and for years I messed myself up with diet pills and diuretics, going for four or five days without food and taking speed or crystal meth (an illegal appetite suppressant). I stopped taking those as well. I just didn't care how I looked."

Not surprisingly, when the five-foot five-inch Delta showed up for the third season fifty pounds heavier—tipping the scales at more than 200 pounds—the press onslaught began, which only made a bad situation worse.

"I went through a *lot* of emotions," she says. "Pain, upset, endless crying, and frustration. I was testy and short-tempered." She also failed to show up for work on occasion, which required juggling schedules and some hasty rewriting. "Luckily," she continues, "the people on the show were wonderful. They talked to me when I needed to talk, and they gave me space when I needed to be alone." Letters from Oprah Winfrey and Elizabeth Taylor were morale boosters, but after a year of constant badgering from the press, Delta says, "I hit the bottom of the barrel. Complete despair. I had total strangers coming up to me in public, ripping open my coat, and saying, 'Hey, lemme see!' Comedians made jokes about me, and reporters staked out my house. I watched years of trying to build a career go down the toilet when I hadn't even done anything wrong!"

What was particularly painful was that she no longer had a crutch to lean on. "In the past, whenever I was down, the one thing I had to fall back on was the fact that people considered me beautiful. Now I didn't even have that. I had nothing, absolutely no self-worth."

In 1989, Delta took more unscheduled time off from the show, not certain "I wanted to be on TV and subjected to that kind of scrutiny." Because of Delta's departure, the press assumed she'd been fired; that wasn't the case. Producer/writer Linda Bloodworth-Thomason insists, "Nothing could have been further from the truth. The pressure was on, and it got to the point where Delta couldn't handle it anymore. It was really affecting her mental state on the show."

During this period, the greatest support came from her husband, actor Gerald McRaney (*Major Dad*), whom she'd met when he played her ex-husband on the show.

"What can I say about him?" Delta says. "Mac kept reassuring me, telling me that he loved me however I looked, and that all this would pass. He was gentle and strong and he helped me realize the truth: that I look like this, and I'm gonna diet, but I can't wait until I'm skinny to start living my life. I started to come back up again. I found my fighting spirit, and I was able to get on with things."

When she returned to the Burbank Studios where the show is shot, she sat down with Linda and the two had a long talk. The result of their chat was a highly praised episode entitled "They Shoot Fat People, Don't They?" in which Delta's character, Suzanne Sugarbaker, goes to her high school reunion much chubbier than she was fifteen years before. There, she overhears comments like, "Suzanne could be poster girl for Save the Whales," and "I heard she's been married many times. Maybe she starved her husbands out." When she's cruelly given an award as the classmate who's changed the most, she bravely accepts and says, "I know I've changed a lot. And when I look around this room, I don't see the receding hairlines or the crow's feet or the potbellies. I just see the beautiful faces of all my friends." Her classmates are moved to applause, and Suzanne makes peace with her inner self while she works on slimming down her outer self.

The episode was cathartic to Delta and to millions of overweight women nationwide; it also helped to earn Delta an Emmy nomination that year.

Today, with the weight coming off slowly thanks to a diet of salads, vegetables, and protein shakes, Delta says, "The hardest thing is to keep going, to stay psyched. I look in the mirror and cry, 'I don't want to look like this!' But eventually, my metabolism will

Heavy Delta hiding behind fellow cast members. From the left: Dixie Carter, Jean Smart, Delta, Meshach Taylor, and Annie Potts. (© Columbia Pictures Television)

change. This time, I'm going to take the weight off *right*."

As Elizabeth Taylor said after losing sixty pounds, "People tend to confuse 'image' with 'self-image.' *Image* refers to our appearance. *Self-image* deals with who we really are." Delta has worked hard to find out who she really is, and her comeback from despair is one of the few tales of triumph in TV Babylon. Unfortunately, she went and blew it after that. Mail and surveys showed that she was the most popular of the actresses on the show, and she wanted more input into her character. Linda Bloodworth-Thomason doesn't give that kind of control. What she gave was support when Delta needed it.

For some inexplicable reason, Delta chose to air her

grievances in the press in an interview in *The Orlando Sentinel*, and Linda was shocked and hurt.

"We have always taken care of Delta," she said. "We loaned her money. We put her in the hospital when she was sick." She also failed to be there for Linda and husband Harry Thomason when they went through personal family crises of their own.

Harry added (in a press release), "Over the past three seasons we have shut down production numerous times because of Delta."

The war of words was on, and it got worse when costar Dixie Carter sided with the Thomasons by issuing a statement that read, in part, that Linda "has not to my knowledge ever said an unkind, aggressive, combative or intentionally hurtful thing to anybody that I know." Dixie's husband, Hal Holbrook, told an interviewer, in essence, that Delta should just collect her paycheck, be grateful for it, and shut up.

Burke responded by going on a *Barbara Walters Special* late in 1990 and sobbing that what "hurt most" about the entire affair was that she "didn't deserve" what Dixie and Hal did "which was to lie and betray me."

In the space of a few months, the atmosphere on the set had gone from one of support and camaraderie (for the few days I was there in early 1990, it was a truly *loving* family) to one that vacillated between curt professionalism and tension. Knowing the justifiable hard-line the Thomasons have taken with their outspoken star, it is unlikely that Delta will grow old and gray on *Designing Women*.

Barr Sinister

She came out of nowhere, or so it seemed. The big, brash, wisecracking, Roseanne and her eponymous TV show debuted on ABC in 1988, produced by Carsey-Werner, the company that brought us *The Cosby Show*.

She was a hit, debuting near the top of the ratings and dethroning Cosby as the number-one show the following year.

She was also put under a microscope by the press—especially what she calls the "tabloid assholes"—and by herself, in the best-selling autobiography. Two different women emerged from each: a spoiled bitch in the press, an ambitious victim in the autobiography. Between both extremes is the real Roseanne. But on this much all sources agree: very few people in TV history have been as seriously affected by the medium, for good and ill, as Roseanne.

Born in Salt Lake City, Utah, in 1952, a Jew among Mormons, Roseanne and her sisters Geraldine and

Stephanie grew up in a tenement owned by her grand-parents. As a child, Roseanne admits that she insisted on being in charge of all activities involving her play-mates: so much so that they nicknamed her "Bossy." However, she says, "I didn't feel then (or now) that hogging all the glory is a disservice. I can do it better than anyone."

When she was sixteen, Roseanne was hit by a car while she was crossing a street. She went up in the air, landed on the hood, and the ornament went into her head. Though the driver claimed that Roseanne was "walking down the middle of the street, begging cars to hit her," Roseanne says she was merely jaywalking.

Regardless, shortly after the accident, Roseanne found that she had difficulty remembering things and suffered recurring dreams that she was paralyzed. Afraid to sleep, she would go for days without it. A doctor prescribed sleeping pills, but that afforded only temporary relief to the fundamental problem; eventually, Roseanne was sent to a state mental institution to deal with her fears. She stayed for eight months, coming home only on weekends. Getting rid of her anxieties, she was out one night in 1971 when she met and fell in love with Bill Pentland, a night clerk at a motor inn. The two were wed and had three children: Jessica, Jennifer, and Jake.

In 1980, tired of sitting at home, Roseanne went to work. She'd always wanted to be "a serious feminist writer," but wasn't sure that books and articles were her medium. The Pentlands were living in Denver at the time and Roseanne got a job in a bar, working as a hostess and waitress. Her quick wit wasn't lost on the male customers and, encouraged by them and by fellow employees, Roseanne jotted down her wry observations about being a mother, housewife, and working woman. Sitting at her typewriter and arranging them into an act, she tried out her material at a local comedy club. She was a hit and, encouraged, boldly headed to Los Angeles, began performing at a local comedy club, and was spotted by a talent scout for *The Tonight Show*. Several on-air appearances followed, after which she was the opening act for Julio Iglesias and also starred in her own cable TV special. Feeling that her self-effacing "domestic goddess" schtick would click with a national audience, Carsey-Warner offered Roseanne her own prime-time network series about a blue-collar family. She jumped at the chance.

The show premiered in the fall of 1988, and if Roseanne thought she'd had problems *before*—

The show as a smash hit and, as in the case of *Moonlighting* and other series that created instant fame, power, and wealth (Roseanne was getting $130,000 an episode), egos didn't just clash on the show, they waged nuclear war.

The first battle was between Roseanne and executive producer Matt Williams, who disagreed about how Roseanne's character should be portrayed. She wanted a lot more anger in her character: Williams and the writers did not. She wanted to deal with important social issues; Williams wanted to do a comedy show. Williams was gone after a few episodes.

Who was to make the necessary script changes? Why, Roseanne's longtime comedian pal Tom Arnold. But Arnold's stuff was awful, and Williams's replacement, Jeff Harris, fired him from his $5,000 a week position. Naturally, this didn't sit well with Roseanne and, come the week of December 4, she decided not to show up for work. Delicate negotiations got her to return, but peace did not come to the set until January of 1990 and Harris's departure. He was replaced by master diplomat Jay Daniel. A veteran of the *Moonlighting* wars, Daniel was billed as co-executive producer; what he was, according to an ABC executive, was "V.P.-Roseanne. If he can keep her in sync, it would justify any salary we have to pay him."

No one doubts that Roseanne was concerned about the scripts and the quality of the show. But she was also on the warpath because of serious personal problems. The greatest catastrophe was the collapse of her fifteen-year-old marriage to Bill Pentland. Actually, it was a rather one-sided collapse at first, since Pentland didn't know a thing about it.

Roseanne has never said why she wanted out of the marriage, but infatuation with Tom Arnold appears to have been the culprit.

The thirty-year-old Arnold had been a friend and confidant since she started in comedy clubs. Roseanne had first contacted him when she found herself having trouble adjusting to series TV—having to *act* instead of simply droning out one-liners. Arnold was helpful and supportive—obviously more so than her husband, who was busy watching the children at their Encino home while Roseanne worked. (And not doing a totally successful job: daughter Jennifer developed a drug problem and, after threatening to kill herself and being placed in CPC Westwood Hospital—a psychiatric institution—she was sent to a detox center in L.A. She is still battling her private demons.)

The relationship with Arnold remained largely on a professional basis and seemed destined to go nowhere

Roseanne Barr with Tom Arnold on *The Oprah Winfrey Show* in 1989. With typical class, Roseanne answers a question about her autobiography *Roseanne: My Life as a Woman.* (AP/Wide World)

when Roseanne headed to New York in March of 1989 to costar with Meryl Streep in the movie *She-Devil*, and Arnold went to work on the comedy club circuit. Overwhelmed by the project and awed to be working with Streep, Roseanne found herself missing Arnold's support and good humor, and wrote letters and poems to him constantly (presumably not of a feminist nature), and phoned regularly. She talked about leaving Pentland and setting up housekeeping with Tom in Beverly Hills. She even offered to buy him a Ferrari.

Arnold winged to New York on April 27.

The couple roomed at the Mayflower Hotel (yes, *that* Mayflower Hotel) and, when Roseanne wasn't working, the two strolled hand-in-hand through adjacent Central Park, dined at local restaurants, and did their best to avoid paparazzi like Ron Galella, who remarked that when the actress first saw them "she was cursing like a trooper and ducking and weaving." (She subsequently calmed down, ignoring the photographers as they snapped away. What love can do to one's peace of spirit!) It should be noted, though, that Roseanne was superkind to most everyone else she encountered, gladly signing autographs for anyone who asked, and being extremely courteous *and* generous to the hotel employees.

Back in Encino, Bill tried to scrape some of the egg off his face.

"I know Tom is with Roseanne," he said. "But there's nothing going on between them."

Or so he thought, until Roseanne began sporting a $12,000 gold-and-diamond engagement ring Arnold had given her. Obviously, things were more serious than even he'd suspected.

But Roseanne's happiness was about to run into a brick wall of a *most* unexpected sort. Following a superb bit of detective work, *The National Enquirer* learned that Roseanne had had an illegitimate daughter in May of 1971—and not by Bill Pentland. After a brief stay at a home for unwed mothers in Denver, Roseanne had given the baby up for adoption. The newspaper found the girl—Brandi Brown, a slender, attractive, well-adjusted, well-liked teenager—living in the upscale Dallas suburb of Richardson, Texas, and attending J.J. Pearce High School.

Upon learning where the girl was, Roseanne phoned and invited her to meet her in Los Angeles. Startled to learn who her mother was, Brandi accepted.

Returning briefly to L.A. on May 25, Roseanne met with Brandi in a $500-a-night suite at the Chateau Marmont—the hotel made infamous when John Belushi died there. Roseanne and Brandi spent the weekend together, after which Brandi returned to Texas . . . and Roseanne further humiliated her husband by staying at Arnold's apartment in Van Nuys—which recently had been vacated by *his* girlfriend, Mara Goodman, who left with most of the furniture after learning about Arnold's activities in New York. "I don't care about the stuff," Arnold told a reporter. "All I really care about is Roseanne."

In the days that followed, the couple was also seen about town, cuddling and kissing openly in elevators and in places like the Backlot Club in West Hollywood. Bill Pentland now had to face the fact that there *was* something going on between Arnold and his wife. When Roseanne returned to New York to finish the film, Bill moved ahead with divorce proceedings. By January 17, the divorce would be final except for certain financial considerations—Pentland wanted $15 million from Roseanne and $3 million from Arnold— as well as the matter of custody, and Roseanne would be free to marry her comedian three days later. For a while, though, it looked as if that wasn't going to happen.

Arnold had a cocaine habit (reported to be $2,000 a week) and a fondness for the bottle, addictions that resulted in violent temper tantrums. During October and November, the double whammy of constant media attention and tension at the show drove him to rely more and more on both substances, which only made matters worse. Ironically, after one day of particularly heavy cocaine use, Arnold started hemorrhaging from the nose and had to be rushed to the hospital. Despite the rumors he was hearing about Arnold and Roseanne, Pentland met him there. Since Arnold had no insurance, Pentland wrote out a check for $5,000 to cover the expenses. Now *that's* a decent guy.

Things came to a head between Arnold and Roseanne a week after Jeff Harris fired the "writer." The hulking Arnold heard the news, then went to Roseanne's dressing room where he threatened to attack the producers. Roseanne tried to calm him, but that only made Arnold angrier. He started yelling at Roseanne, asking whose side she was on, and she began screaming back, shouting that the wedding was off and she wanted Arnold out of her life. Then she called for security personnel, who came quickly and grabbed Arnold. Arnold struggled, but was in no condition to put up much of a fight; seeing his pitiful condition, Roseanne decided to have him taken right to Century City Hospital and placed in a drug detoxification program. Then she issued a terse statement to the press: "My Jan. 20 marriage to Tom Arnold is off."

A few days later, Roseanne canceled five concert performances she was to give at the Circle Star Center in San Carlos, California. "Her doctor has insisted that in order to preserve her health, she reschedule all current engagements," said a spokesperson. Roseanne was exhausted, physically and emotionally, a condition not helped by the box office failure of the truly terrible *She-Devil*.

As 1989 drew to a close, Roseanne wondered how

things could possibly have gone so wrong. She had no beau, no husband, no privacy, no film career. Even her hit show wasn't what it *should* have been. Not only was it like Iwo Jima on the set, but although *Roseanne* was the most popular show on television, ratings didn't climb the way they do for most hit shows in their sophomore years. Industry analysts attributed the stagnation to the bad press Roseanne had received: not just the big, tawdry stories but incidents involving mooning at a baseball game (showing the world Tom's name tattooed on her derriere during a 1989 World Series game), Roseanne renting pornographic tapes at a video store, Arnold paying a pair of thugs fifty dollars to beat up photographers outside the L.A. nightspot Spago, and other vile doings that turned off huge portions of the audience.

Roseanne hid out in Hawaii during Christmas and New Year's, and Bill took the kids to Colorado. While Roseanne was away, she relaxed, cleared her head, and decided to give Arnold another chance if he could straighten himself out. The stay in detox seemed to work and, on January 16, Roseanne decided to go ahead with plans to wed Arnold four days later. The marriage took place at Roseanne's rented Benedict Canyon mansion, after which the couple flew to Acapulco for a honeymoon.

For a while, it seemed as if Roseanne's life and career had stablized. Then she got into a feud with talk-show host Arsenio Hall, who made a couple of fat-cracks about Roseanne on his show. Roseanne retaliated a few days later on March 10, 1990, by suggesting during the *American Comedy Awards* that Arsenio and Jim Nabors are lovers (remarks that were edited from the taped broadcast of the event). Arsenio replied with a haymaker on his program, "Jim Nabors? Hmmm . . . I'd still make out better than Tom Arnold did."

It was quiet for a few months after that, and then—disaster. The worst one yet.

One of the producers of her show, Tom Werner, is also managing general partner of the San Diego Padres baseball team. To get some publicity for his club and the TV show both, he asked Roseanne to sing the national anthem before the second game of a doubleheader on July 25, 1990.

When Roseanne walked out onto the field, *boy* did he get publicity. Only not the kind he wanted.

Roseanne sang an off-key, screeching rendition of *The Star-Spangled Banner*, and almost at once the booing started. Roseanne later said that when she heard the shouts, "I went into this panic thing, and I thought, 'Can I quit?' But I couldn't. It took all the guts in my life to finish that song."

But then she did something even more unfortunate. As if the singing hadn't been insulting enough, when she finished, she grabbed her crotch and spit. She was *trying* to parody what baseball players do all the time—but, due to the timing of the gestures, succeeded only in insulting the anthem. Roseanne left this field of nightmares to the boos and hisses of 30,000 fans. Padres pitcher Eric Show summed up everyone's feelings when he said, "It's an insult—there are people who died for that song." Even President Bush got into the act, calling her actions "disgraceful." The Padres switchboard received more than 2,000 calls protesting Barr's interpretation of the anthem.

After the game, an Associated Press reporter called

the star at home. Roseanne refused to come to the phone, and Tom told the reporter, "They knew what kind of singer she is. She's just an average singer . . . not an opera singer." He added that she was "very sorry. She's very upset that people think she meant disrespect."

Criticism snowballed—*The New York Post* ran a next-day headline, BARR-F!—and Roseanne realized she needed to do some damage control. She appeared on an L.A. TV news show and also held a press conference to explain that she meant no disrepsect. "I apologize that people were so appalled," she said. She then explained, "The players and my husband said: 'Why don't you scratch yourself and spit like all the players do?' I may have done it a little too close to *The Star Spangled Banner.*"

That was an understatement.

However, Roseanne couldn't resist taking a dig at her critics by noting, "If this is the worst thing they ever heard, they've had it really easy."

Incredibly, after two years in the prime-time spotlight, Roseanne still hadn't realized that she must deal with a heterogeneous national audience differently than she would a comedy club following. They're not as thick-skinned or tolerant, and while they'll overlook behind-baring eccentricities, they won't stand for insults or mockery.

Tom Werner knew that, and the Padres immediately issued an apologetic statement, concluding it by saying that "in the future we will strive to see that the anthem is presented with the dignity it is due." The next night, they had a Marine band come in and do the job right.

A few days after the imbroglio, Roseanne appeared

on *The Sally Jessy Raphael Show* and, during the course of her interview, sang a far more heartfelt version of the anthem. Her remorse *was* sincere, but the damage was already done: sponsors withdrew from the show, the series took a ratings nosedive, and there were death threats—one of which, a warning that she'd be shot, drove Roseanne to tears during an appearance on Rick Dees' *Into the Night* show.

Because tensions were so high, Roseanne and Tom left town. When they returned on August 5, they did it in typical Roseanne-and-Tom style: when photographers spotted the duo and started taking pictures, Tom went wild. Photographer Gary Lewis says, "Tom just snapped and ran toward me. I turned my back toward him to protect my film, and he punched me in the back as hard as he could. The pain was excruciating."

Tom tackled Gary and ripped the strobe from his camera, while Roseanne urged her husband on. But when he *really* started tearing into the photographer, Roseanne suddenly changed her mind and shouted, "Tom, don't do that! Let's get out of here."

The combative couple walked toward the elevator where they encountered two other photographers. One, Bob Scott, says, "As Roseanne saw Ralph snapping pictures, she turned to Tom and said, 'Get him too, honey.' " Tom obliged, going after shutterbug Ralph Dominguez first. When Tim finished destroying *his* flash, he threw it at Scott, hitting him in the groin, then ran over and pounded him, ripping off his shirt and, as Scott puts it, "clawing at me and slugging me in the face and thighs. He kicked me in the leg and slugged me in the mouth before walking away."

Charges were pressed, and the matter is pending.

None of this, however, has soured Roseanne on her knight in shining armor. One of her New Year's resolutions for 1991 was to change her *nom de theatre:* she told the press that come the fall, the star of *Roseanne* would be listed in the credits as Roseanne Arnold. It was a nice, homey, well-meaning touch . . . although neither that nor print ads stressing the show's hearth-and-family values helped to put the brakes on its dramatic ratings slide.

Roseanne may be the prime example of a potentially tremendous talent destroyed by success. She was moved along too fast, never acquiring the maturity or savvy needed to handle fame and money—a not inconsiderable $150,000 a week plus 15 percent of her show's profits. Like a green soldier thrown against a seasoned enemy, all the support and artillery in the world hasn't been enough to save her from her worst foe: herself.

Savitch Innocence

Failure is relative. Whatever her blunders, at least Roseanne is still alive; not everyone is so fortunate.

In Philadelphia, Jessica Savitch was a hero, a bright young woman who'd made good, who'd triumphed in a man's world. And she hadn't made it solely on good looks, either.

Unlike most of the newsreaders on local newscasts, Jessica Savitch of KWY-TV's *Eyewitness News* had presence and authority, eyes that burned with intelligence. It didn't matter that she had a slight lisp, that the phrase, "Spring has sprung" came out as "Shpring has shprung" during one broadcast. The flaw only made the cool professional more accessible, more like us. Off camera, to see her address a group or give a speech at a function was a lesson in poise and charisma.

Jessica came to KWY in 1974 after spending three years at KHOU in Houston. By 1977, NBC news had come calling, and she went to Washington to host the network's prestigious minute-long prime-time *NBC News Digest* updates, and anchor the Saturday edition of *NBC Nightly News.*

Market research indicated that she was one of the best-liked newscasters. Unfortunately, she was also the most troubled. Behind the clean, farm-girl good looks and solid professionalism was a human catastrophe.

Savitch was ambitious but insecure. As one of her coworkers expressed it—perfectly—"She was always living on the next page." Because she wasn't able to deal with the pressure or get away from it, tantrums on the set were a common occurrence, even in the Philadelphia days, caused by everything from the pages of her script being handed to her out of order to the temperature in the studio being too hot or cold for her.

Compounding her problems—and, more and more, causing them—was Jessica's addiction to cocaine. Because sex wasn't that important to her, she'd started using the drug in the early 1970s as an aphrodisiac. When she was on cocaine, she became uninhibited, able to satisfy her partner . . . and herself. Before long, she was using it to stay awake on the job (she once said that stamina was a broadcast newsperson's most important asset), and was also regularly downing amphetamines.

Unfortunately, Jessica's drug-enhanced sex life did not help her achieve satisfaction in her personal relationships. She met older advertising executive Melvin Robert Korn, a generous, pampering father figure, and wed him on January 6, 1980. Mel sued for divorce in November, alarmed by Jessica's increasing reliance on drugs and her almost manic preoccupation with her career. As if that weren't upsetting enough, Jessica had had an abortion during the marriage, a decision that tortured her. She'd already had one in 1974, after a fling with a friend left her pregnant; although Jessica desperately wanted a child to love, she couldn't stand the thought of anything interrupting her career. Still, in both cases, the guilt never went away, along with the desire to have a baby.

Jessica consoled herself after the failed marriage by taking up with her Washington gynecologist Donald Rollie Payne. It was an ill-advised, on-the-rebound relationship for them both with Jessica as the driving force: when she got pregnant for a third time, she told Payne that she was going to have the baby, and it would look bad for them both if they weren't married. The doctor felt shanghaied, but on March 21, 1981, they were wed, Payne moving through the ceremony and reception as though he were in a daze.

Or stoned.

Shortly after the nuptials, Jessica discovered that Payne's use of drugs exceeded her own, probably including hard substances as well. Fearing that any Payne/Savitch child would suffer from a bad gene mix and two troubled parents, she had another abortion.

On August 2, Jessica returned to Washington after a trip to New York. When she reached the house, she was unable to find Payne: she finally looked in the basement and found him hanging from a ceiling beam in the laundry room, the leash of Jessica's dog Chewy knotted around his neck. His tongue was hanging out, his eyes were bugged and bleeding, his flesh was white, and his hands were swollen with blood.

Jessica ran from the house, screaming for help.

She transferred to New York shortly thereafter, but

never recovered from this ultimate rejection. She became more reliant on drugs and pills, grew arrogant and even more driven than before, and was utterly unable to relax. As NBC news anchor Tom Brokaw put it, "She was wound just tighter than a two-dollar clock."

The professional destruction of Jessica Savitch followed the personal one. On October 3, 1983, she went on the air just before 9:00 P.M. to do the *NBC News Digest* segment. Her words were slurred and mumbled, she hesitated, her expression was alternately mystified and terror-stricken. She later blamed it on the wine she had had at dinner, and a faulty Tele-PrompTer. But everyone at NBC knew the truth: she was so coked up she couldn't think straight.

Her dreams of eventually landing the evening news anchor desk ended that night. Rival Connie Chung's star was rising at the network, and this flub was all Jessica had needed to self-destruct. It took less than a minute for the years of hard work to go down the drain.

And yet, there was still a hint of hope. A few days before the debacle, she'd gone on a date with a man two years her junior, Martin Fischbein, a savvy, successful executive at *The New York Post*. He'd contacted Jessica through a mutual friend, they'd had a great time on their date, and they agreed to go out again, on a drive to Bucks County in Pennsylvania, to visit places in and around Kennett Square, where Jessica had grown up. Jessica was looking forward to having the time with Fischbein, being able to talk to him about the debacle.

It was raining on Sunday, October 23, when the couple and Jessica's Siberian husky Chewy set out from New York in a rented blue Oldsmobile station wagon. Because of the weather, by the time they reached New Hope, Pennsylvania, they decided to stop and spend the day at the quaint shops in the artists' colony. They had dinner at Chez Odette, an old haunt of Jessica's; in fact, the restaurant had made the news in May of 1977, while Jessica was at KWY. A man, Caron Ehehalt, had eaten there, driven out of parking lot in a storm, thought the path in the back was an exit, and plunged into the waters of the adjoining Delaware Canal, where he drowned.

The couple finished eating around 7:00 P.M., then walked out to the car. It was foggy when Jessica got in the backseat to hug Chewy. Fischbein buckled his seat belt and backed slowly from the parking spot. Then he drove ahead, still traveling slowly, to the dirt slope, which he thought would take him to the canal bridge. He inched ahead, barely able to see in the driving rain, fog, and blackness; in the dark, he had missed the two large signs on either side of the path that said MOTOR VEHICLES PROHIBITED. He continued forward slowly, traveling fifty feet along the leaf-covered path.

Ahead, Fischbein saw spotlights. Due to the late hour and weather, he could not have known that they were on the side of a house on the other side of the canal, not on the road. He also saw a flashing yellow light, and apparently assumed that it adjoined the parking lot exit. Again, he would have had no way of knowing that it abutted the canal.

Seeing all the lights, Fischbein accelerated slightly. There was no fence along the canal—there was nothing but a sheer drop off a stone wall, the top of which was level with the ground. In the dark, if he saw the canal at all, he could very well have mistaken its dark surface for a road.

He turned toward it, and the station wagon went right over the wall. It flipped over as it fell, and dropped ten feet before landing upside down in water three feet deep, with four feet of mud below that. The roof struck a log and caved in so that a deep V ran down the center from front to back.

Fischbein was killed instantly. Despite having struck the roof of the car and suffering a head injury, however, Savitch was conscious. Mud, water, and debris were pouring through the broken back windshield; disoriented, unable to see the shattered window through which she might have crawled free, Savitch instead kicked desperately against the rear doors. But the crushed roof and thick mud in which they'd settled made it impossible to get them open.

Savitch didn't stop pushing until the entire inside of the car was filled with mud. Death came from drowning; she died with her knees against her chest, eyes open. She was a month shy of her thirty-sixth birthday.

The car went unnoticed until nearly five hours later, when Sharon and John Nyari, the people who owned the house on the other side of the canal, came home. It wasn't until the bodies were taken to the morgue and the mud cleaned away that their identities became known. At the scene, rescue team member Mario Lasarro noted with sadness that if it hadn't been for the mud, Savitch "probably would have been able to get out."

Jessica and Chewy were cremated. Six months later, Savitch's estate filed a wrongful death suit against eight parties, including the *Post*'s parent company and

Jessica Savitch's dog Chewy, in a body bag, lies beside the car in which the newscaster drowned. Note the spotlights in the background, lights that helped lead Jessica to her death. (AP/Wide World, Eric Silverman)

the restaurant. In February 1988, the estate settled out of court for $8.15 million.

If it's not quite true that Jessica Savitch was on the verge of getting her life together, it *is* fair to say that the potential was there. The shock of what had happened on the air seemed to have opened her eyes to

two things: that she was going to have to work hard
to regain the credibility she'd lost among viewers and
coworkers, and that dumping drugs had to be part of
that. She was really working on it: in the investigation
that followed her death, no drugs were found in the
car, nor in the two bodies. The alcohol content in
their blood was extremely low. Jessica had been able
to be herself with Fischbein—a sign that the relationship had potential.

CBS newsman Charles Osgood called television an
"alluring trap" for Jessica Savitch, a powerful magnet
for someone with her looks, intelligence, and ambition. The real tragedy, though, is not the trap itself,
but that after years of struggle, Jessica was finally
close to beating it.

Here Today, Gone Tomorrow

Once in a rare while, the good guys win in TV Babylon.

Forty-year-old Jane Pauley is a confident, smart woman who hasn't lost her unpretentious, youthful, self-effacing spirit. Everyone who has followed her career agrees that thirteen years of cohosting *The Today Show* turned her from a ponytailed novice into a poised professional. Yet it took the crude, humiliating matter of her departure from the program to *really* mature her, to give her what she calls her "new-found courage."

When we met at Jane's NBC offices in Rockefeller Center a few weeks after her resignation, she was dressed conservatively in a gray jacket and skirt with a light gray blouse. Class, not flash. As we talked, Jane's smile was sincere, her eyes trusting, her manner so friendly and lacking in pretense—in short, she was so *likable*—that the temptation was strong to boycott NBC for having caused her a moment's grief.

Before discussing the assault on Jane and her remarkable apotheosis, some history.

After graduating from Indiana University, Jane was hired in 1972 as a reporter on local WISH-TV, then went to Chicago in 1975 to co-anchor the news at WMAQ-TV. A year later she was tapped to replace Barbara Walters on *Today*. It was a quick ascension, and though Jane was criticized for being relatively inexperienced, just a pretty face, viewers loved her. She quickly became a first-rate interviewer and *really* surprised her detractors in 1980 when she married intellectual *Doonesbury* creator Garry Trudeau, whom she'd met at a dinner at Tom Brokaw's house. Obviously, there was more to this woman than just a fast, friendly smile and a pleasant manner.

Cut to August of 1989. *The Today Show* was suffering from a small ratings erosion, and that was preying on Jane. When she enrolled her twins Ross and Rachel in kindergarten (a son, Thomas, was born in 1986), she says she began to realize that "a phase of my life was ending. So I wondered if it was also time for a professional change." She adds that she was afraid to remain on the *Today* program for fear of being known as "a one-trick pony."

Jane and Garry took a vacation and she thought about her career. What happened surprised her. Instead of convincing herself that it was time to leave the show, she found herself "reinvigorated." She says, "The thought of change can do that to you. I didn't have this killer ambition to be a solo act, and I accepted the fact that I was happy and comfortable being a member of a team."

Upon returning from her little holiday, Jane met

with NBC executives and told them she'd had this minor crisis, but it had passed. She was ready to do what she could to help the show. That's when the executives hit *her* with a dirty little surprise of their own. They'd decided to try and woo younger viewers by unceremoniously dumping seasoned news anchor John Palmer, age fifty-three, and replacing him with thirty-one-year-old beauty Deborah Norville, a former co-anchor (ironically) at WMAQ and lately the news anchor on the *Sunrise* program. So much for loyalty to a devoted employee.

Jane felt sorry for Palmer and had a faint feeling of could-it-happen-to-me? But objectively, she had no problem with NBC's idea. "I've always been a good team player," she says, "and I want to play on the winning team." If Norville could boost the ratings, Jane was all for it.

But NBC didn't tell Jane *everything*. What she didn't realize was that Norville would be sitting on the couch beside her and cohost Bryant Gumbel at the beginning and end of the show. That prominence, plus Norville's $1 million a year salary—close to the $1.2 million veteran Jane was earning—created the impression that someone was on the way out. And it wasn't Gumbel. (Gumbel, incidentally, was already earning *twice* what Jane was making. Was he worth it? Read on.)

"NBC wasn't trying to force me out," Jane insists. "I'm not being naive about that: they didn't want to destroy what made the *Today* program work, they just wanted to add something to that. They assumed that because I had thirteen years of momentum and a certain reputation, Deborah's arrival wouldn't be regarded as an assault on my position."

But the press and public felt that it was *precisely* that, and the ivory-tower dwellers at NBC—specifically NBC president Robert Wright, NBC News president Michael Gartner, and *Today* show chief Dick Ebersol—did nothing to change that impression. They couldn't have *bought* the kind of publicity the controversy was generating and, by their cruel, self-serving silence, the network only encouraged speculation about Jane's bleak future.

If Jane came off looking like a patsy, the press was absolutely merciless with Gumbel. His appeal had already taken a hammering in February of 1989 with the leak of a memo he'd written, which was highly critical of weatherman Willard Scott, among others (though not Jane). Now, he was being damaged further by the perception that he'd forced Jane out in order to bring in Norville, over whom he would have seniority and a relative amount of control. That would have given him all the juicy assignments and made *The Today Show*, in essence, *The Bryant Gumbel Show*. Surveys indicated that his popularity with viewers wasn't so high that he could weather that kind of bad publicity. One viewer summed up everyone's feelings best when she wrote in a letter to the tabloid *Globe*, "Bryant Gumbel is nothing but a pompous fool."

As rough as things were for Gumbel, however, the media was even harder on Norville. The Knight-Ridder newspapers charged her with having "bad karma." *Newsweek* wrote, "If he (Ebersol) thinks hiring Norville at the expense of Pauley will appeal to the ladies, he may be in for a big surprise. This isn't *Working Girl*." The lofty *Manhattan, Inc.*, charged that "Deborah Norville is as much a journalist as Dan Quayle is a vice president," and *Good Housekeeping* noted that "in today's competitive TV environment, Norville would not have had a prayer of getting where she is if she weren't good looking."

Not surprisingly, the tabloids also got in their licks, most notably *The Star*, in which Norville's ex-boy-friend, former footballer Harmon Wages, quoted Norville as having said that once she got to *Sunrise*, "I'll give the midget (Pauley) six months."

At first, Jane says she didn't hurt for herself but for both of her coworkers. That's not just lip service: she's *that* kind of person. "I felt real awkward about the fact that Deborah and I were viewed to be in competition for my job, and that people thought Bryant was manipulating events behind the scenes. Those accusations simply weren't true. Bryant and I are very, very good friends. He can be cocky sometimes, but he also possesses humility and vulnerability. And Deborah was *happy* to be where she was . . . until the press started roasting her.

"You want to know what I think of Deborah? I hold her up as a standard of excellence. I really do. What she was subjected to was extreme. If it had been me getting all that criticism, I would *not* have been functioning professionally. I probably wouldn't have even wanted to show my face."

Despite her empathy, though, Jane was also angry at NBC for their ham-fisted handling of the affair. The doubts she'd had about continuing on the show came raging back, and this time she didn't suppress them.

"I asked myself if I could *really* follow through,"

she says, "and I was surprised and pleased at my readiness to make the change. You have to understand, that was a big thing for me. I never went into the boss's office and pounded my fist on the desk, saying, 'Give me more money! Give me a prime-time show!' Going to the network and telling them I was leaving was a big step."

She grins as she thinks back to the support her husband gave her when she announced she was going to leave the show.

"Oh, Garry was fully supportive . . . once the color returned to his face," she says with a laugh. "The truth is, it's well known in my household that the advice my husband gave me was pretty bad. His initial reaction to NBC's handling of the whole thing was slash and burn. I remember him telling someone that most people in my position would have left tire tracks on Deborah's back. Garry's not mean, but he was concerned because he loves me, because my career is important to him, and because he didn't want to see me hurt."

When Jane went in and announced her decision on October 27, the network was stunned. As former NBC reporter Linda Ellerbee puts it, "They want people who are skeptical and questioning as professionals, but they really want you to be very docile as a person." The network was also worried—make that terrified—because early surveys showed that Norville was perceived as a homewrecker and may actually have been hurting the show. Gumbel's popularity was also charting *extremely* low.

Suddenly fearful that Jane would defect to another network, NBC began backpedaling, wooing her in every way imaginable. The deal NBC came up with was unprecedented: Jane got a $400,000 raise, was asked to host five prime-time specials (ratings hits that were later spun off into a weekly series, *Real People*), and was given the prestigious spot as substitute anchor for Tom Brokaw on the *Nightly News*. Not bad for a woman who, just a few weeks before, seemed to have a future as bright as old Coke when new Coke was introduced.

"No, not bad at all," Jane agrees with a little smile—the smile of the cat that swallowed the mouse.

Ironically, after Jane left *The Today Show* in December, the ratings no longer eroded, they collapsed. They've continued falling catastrophically ever

On her last day as a *Today* show cohost, Jane Pauley presents replacement Deborah Norville with an alarm clock. Moments later, the two women embraced. (AP/Wide World)

since, and the loss to NBC in advertising revenue has been staggering: $100,000 *a day!* Not only that, but although viewing habits can be shocked into change by the dismissal of an anchor, audiences tend to stay put otherwise. Viewers who have defected to ABC's *Good Morning America* and *CBS This Morning* will not be coming back until *those* shows make a change. The hasty addition of old favorite Joe Garagiola to *The Today Show* desk in the summer of 1990 barely helped the ratings.

In short, Deborah Norville was not long for the world of *Today*. When she became pregnant in 1990, cynics felt she'd have the baby then *stay* home, giving her a face-saving way to leave the show.

And that's more or less what happened. Her "temporary" replacement, personable Katherine Couric, caused the ratings to shoot to their pre-Norville levels. As a result, on April 4, NBC announced that Couric would be sticking around and that Norville would not . . . though the banished cohost could take some solace in the multimillion dollar settlement it took to settle her five-year, no-cut contract. At home with her son Niki, Norville summed up her experiences as "a real character builder that I wouldn't wish on my worst enemy."

Though the NBC fiasco has resolved itself with a minimum of bloodshed, Pauley is still rather glum about the future of women in TV news. "Women have a big problem. Because of their good looks, they're easily marketable and are tempted very young to take prestigious, highly paid anchor jobs instead of paying their dues as reporters. Then they're criticized for a lack of experience."

She has no suggestion on how to change that, and doesn't believe it *will* change. As Deborah Norville learned, in TV Babylon it's possible to reach for the brass ring, get it . . . and still fall off the carousel.

Raggedy Andy

Jane Pauley was a newsperson who got into trouble she didn't ask for. Conversely, *60 Minutes* commentator Andy Rooney fell into a snake pit of his own making, a victim of his characteristic candor.

Born in 1920, Rooney worked as a reporter for the military newspaper *Stars and Stripes* during World War II. After the war, he worked as a writer for radio and TV, penning scripts for Arthur Godfrey, Garry Moore, and the CBS news series *The Twentieth Century*, among others. He became an on-air commentator for *60 Minutes* in 1978, highly regarded for his fresh, sarcastic looks at everything from sacred cows to small inconsistencies in our daily lives.

Off-camera, Rooney's ready tongue incurred the wrath of his bosses several times during his tenure on the show. In 1986, he slammed network management for layoffs that he felt were detrimental to the news division. The following year, he was suspended without pay for refusing to cross a writers' picket line.

In October of 1989, he got the ball rolling on what were to be his most controversial actions by writing in his syndicated column, "I feel the same way about homosexuals as I do about cigarette smokers—I wouldn't want to spend much time in a small room with one."

Gay leaders were understandably upset with Rooney, who made things even worse on December 20, 1989. During a special year-end summary of events, *A Year With Andy Rooney: 1989,* Rooney blamed the ills of the world on, "Too much alcohol, too much food, drugs, homosexual unions, cigarettes."

Gay leaders were justifiably outraged, and they met with CBS officials to protest. Network executives agreed to sponsor gay sensitivity talks for the news staff, but refused to consider any kind of disciplinary actions against Rooney.

For his part, Rooney conceded that his comments about too many "homosexual unions" on the year-end show were ill-advised. What he should have said, he admitted, was "too much unsafe sex."

In an effort to soothe hurt feelings and hopefully clarify his ideas in an appropriate forum, Rooney gave an interview to the gay magazine *The Advocate.* That only caused things to go from bad to godawful: in the February 27, 1990, issue (the contents of which were leaked three weeks early), Rooney was reported to have said that he feels sorry for gays, adding, "But I still don't think it's normal. I think that homosexuality is inherently dangerous."

Even worse, the article quoted him as saying this about blacks: "I've believed all along that most people are born with equal intelligence, but blacks have watered down their genes because the less intelligent ones are the ones that have the most children."

When the magazine appeared, Rooney immediately declared that he was misquoted. "Anyone who knows me knows I'm not racist," he said. "I did not say, nor would I have thought that. It is an idiotic statement to have made; I would not have made it in a million years." He says that what he told the reporter was, "If you go to West Virginia or Georgia you find a lot of white kids are dropping out, and the kids with the least education are having the most babies." He says that he made it very clear to the reporter that he was not making a racial statement, but "a class statement."

Rooney was furious that his integrity and intelligence were being questioned, a sentiment echoed by veteran newsman Walter Cronkite and many other coworkers. Rooney said that he felt he was "the victim of a gay conspiracy. CBS had turned down a gay demand to fire me. The gays knew the only way they could get me was to claim I was a racist."

Whether or not that was true (the quotes were not tape-recorded, so it's impossible to know exactly what Rooney said), the damage had been done. Andy was fired—but Mike Wallace and Ed Bradley (who is black) protested vigorously, and the CBS brass backed down. Instead, on February 8, they suspended him without pay for three months. Moreover, the network said (but did not really mean) that after the suspension, his future with the show was not 100 percent assured.

As soon as the action was announced, CBS received 2,594 calls from viewers, 2,549 of which opposed the suspension. CBS held fast. Then, a more important voice was heard: the ratings. A whopping 20 percent of the audience tuned out. Meanwhile, other potential employers made overtures to Rooney, from Fox network owner Rupert Murdoch to Tampa's small WFLA-AM, which wanted him to host an afternoon radio show.

While Rooney twiddled his thumbs, the ratings of *60 Minutes* stayed down and CBS earned millions of dollars less than they would have ordinarily.

To no one's surprise, on March 4, less than a month after his unceremonious suspension, Rooney was back on the air. The ratings not only returned to their former glory but were actually *higher* than in the weeks before the suspension.

Looking back on the matter, Rooney said of gays, "I understand more than I did before this happened. I believe they are in a more difficult position than I understood. I recognize more than I did before."

In that respect, the entire matter hadn't been for naught. However, as Andy pointed out in his return commentary, "Do I have any opinions that might irritate some people? You're damn right I do. That's what I'm here for." And in an address that May to 1,000 people at a Constitutional Rights Foundation dinner, he complained bitterly that "my suspension was a better example of timidity in broadcasting than it was a violation of my First Amendment rights." In that same speech he also decried, "the timidity with which the broadcast industry approaches seriously controversial ideas."

Regardless of who was right or wrong, the bottom line really is this. CBS suspended Rooney because it feared black backlash and advertiser retaliation. It reinstated him when viewers defected and advertising revenue fell accordingly. In both cases, it was money and not principle that guided the news division.

That, more than anything, is the real news—and the real crime.

Rather Unfortunate

Vice-President Spiro Agnew once railed against the anchorpeople of TV news, criticizing them as "a tiny, enclosed fraternity of privileged men elected by no one," people who used "a raised eyebrow, an inflection of the voice, a caustic remark" to give a little twist to what was *supposed* to be an objective newscast.

Agnew was a partisan hit man. If the Nixon White House hadn't been taking criticism from the network news, the vice president wouldn't have had a complaint in the world.

Though Agnew was ultimately disgraced, more and more politicians and conservative spokespeople began taking up his gauntlet, especially in the Reagan era. And the prime target for their wrath was a newsman who is, in fact, a liberal—but also happens to be better read and more intelligent than virtually all of his critics.

It's fitting that the book end with his story. For he

is, in many ways, the best example of a public figure who was battered, over and over, by TV and his critics, yet survived—armor dented, but his pride intact.

Truth be told, Dan Rather *is* a curious fellow. If you spend any amount of time with him, you'll meet three distinctly different people. The first is the affable, somewhat rigid figure the public sees each night on *The CBS Evening News*. That one's a fake. The second is also a phony, the man people meet in the street—the one who looks like Dick Tracy or Humphrey Bogart in *Casablanca*, his six-foot, two-inch frame hunched inside a trench coat, his movie-star handsome features hidden behind a floppy fedora. He greets people in a low monotone, anxious *not* to be recognized. In fact, he admits, "I'm somewhat awkward about the celebrity side of this business. It's my nature to be friendly, but people tend to want to discuss the issues, and if you do too much of that, you lose precious time for journalism." People who erroneously call him standoffish forget that he's not a TV actor, not a mere celebrity, but a working reporter. He's got a lot to do, every day.

Then there's the third Dan Rather, the one who isn't performing or hiding. This one is a soft-spoken, scrupulously courteous, instantly likable family man whose greatest vice is "drinking enough coffee to float a horseshoe." This is the Dan Rather who has one great fear, and one only: "Being mediocre. I *hate* mediocrity."

Rather is a hard worker and an intellectual. He can quote Tolstoy, Yeats, or the *Bible*—a dog-earned copy of which is always handy in his office, and is read with some frequency. Recreational reading is the likes of *Decisive Battles of the World* by Sir Edward Creasy, published in 1851. For Rather, it's more than just the thrill of learning new things that attracts him to history. Throughout his many ordeals, past and present, he draws strength from the fact that, "As it did after the Battle of Syracuse, when the Athenians were trapped in the harbor, all sieges end and life goes on."

Born in Wharton, Texas, in 1931, Rather majored in journalism at a small teacher's college, spent time in the Marines, then went to work at Houston radio station KTRH. Shifting to TV, he became anchor of the CBS Houston affiliate KHOU-TV. In 1961, his coverage of Hurricane Carla—from the very heart of the storm—earned him national attention. Two years later, he was instrumental in CBS's coverage of the assassination of President Kennedy.

Over the years, Rather has found himself in the midst of danger. In 1955, he had a Houston police officer inject him with heroin so he could do a story about its effects. "The experience was a special kind of hell," he says. "I came out understanding full well how one could be addicted—and quickly." While covering the civil rights movement in the South, he was once beaten with a rifle butt. On another occasion, he had a sawed-off shotgun pushed into his ribs and he probably would have been killed if a CBS employee had not broken Rather's own rule and been packing a gun, which he used to force the assailant off. While covering the 1968 Democratic National Convention in Chicago, he was punched on-camera by a security guard. ("He lifted me right off the floor and put me away. I was getting to my feet when Walter came to me with a question.")

But Rather kept coming back for more because the news is *important* to him. He wants to get the truth

out to people. As a result, Rather earned a reputation
for being tough and aggressive, but he didn't really
get into trouble with the political right until he became
the White House correspondent. At the height of
Watergate, Rather (along with other reporters covering the event) was warned by people protecting the
president to play down the affair. Rather did not
oblige and, as a result, received threatening calls late
at night, found people watching his home from the
shadows, and had prowlers in his office, going through
his files for names of sources.

Bad as that was, it got worse. On a fateful day in
1974, during a presidential press conference, he stood
to ask Richard Nixon a question. As soon as Rather
rose, there was a mixture of applause and boos; the
soon-to-be-ex-president asked Rather, "Are you running for something?"

Rather shot back, "No, sir, Mr. President. Are
you?"

His jibe couldn't have made him a bigger target for
the right if he'd painted concentric red circles on his
chest.

Rather saw the Nixon presidency through and,
when it was all over, left the White House and became
part of the *60 Minutes* team. But associates did a lot
of the research there and, in April of 1980, restless
for some of the old hands-on reporting, he put on
peasant garb, flew to Afghanistan, and did a ballsy
report from behind enemy lines. He was stung by subsequent criticism that he was grandstanding: Rather
and his crew had gone into the heart of battle, and
stood as good a chance of being shot as the locals
fighting the Russians. By this time, though, there was
another reason for the anti-Rather sentiment in the

air: CBS had just named him to replace Walter Cronkite, "the most trusted man in television," as anchor of *The CBS Evening News*.

"It's a good thing I love a challenge," Rather says, "because Walter is concerned and poised and has a wealth of inner integrity. To follow a man like that was both flattering and intimidating."

And humbling. Starting off a decade of trouble for Rather was an erosion in the ratings. Cronkite had always handily dominated the evening newscasts; Rather did not. Many critics and viewers regarded him as too intense, and the producers tried to soften him up by tucking him into wool cardigans, making him speak slowly, and smile more. All that the image-makers managed, however, to do was make Rather seem *uncomfortable*. They left him alone, and let him dress himself.

As it happens, when Tom Brokaw took over the news anchor desk at NBC in 1982, *he* fared even worse. What hurt both Rather and Brokaw was Peter Jennings over at ABC. He isn't half the newsman Rather is, but he radiates warmth and sincerity. That's what many viewers want at dinnertime to make the bad news go down a little easier.

As if Rather weren't hounded enough by charges that he was no Walter Cronkite, he was embarrassed by something that happened in Chicago on November 10, 1980. Rather got in a cab and, when the driver couldn't find the address, Rather refused to pay the $12 fare. The hack, in turn, took Rather for a rollercoasterlike ride down Lake Shore Drive. Opening the window, Rather shouted incongruously, "I'm being kidnapped!" An off-duty corrections officer heard his cries and was able to stop the cab.

Dan Rather, following along as a deposition is quoted in the case of *Dr. Carl Galloway* vs. *60 Minutes*. (UPI/Bettmann)

If one were inclined to look for symbolism, that wild cab ride was a metaphor for the years to come.

Except for testimony in May of 1983 in a slander suit brought against *60 Minutes* by Dr. Carl Galloway of Lynwood, California, things were quiet for a while. The ratings stablized as viewers discovered that what Rather was giving them was *news*, not the candy-coated "infotainment" being handed out at ABC. (The harder issues were generally left for Ted Koppel on *Nightline*.)

Rather finally appeared to hit his stride when he stumbled into a series of events that portrayed him as either hapless or carnivorous, neither of which he is.

The first occurred in New York City on October 4, 1986. Rather was walking down Park Avenue, heading to this apartment on 75th Street after dining at the apartment of friend and CBS coworker David Buksbaum. It was 10:45, and Rather had just reached 88th Street when he was approached by a man in a dark suit. He was a white man, in his thirties, about six feet tall with dark hair and a mustache. The newcomer stood in front of Rather and asked the now-infamous question, "Kenneth, what is the frequency?"

Rather was confused, and replied politely, "I beg your pardon. I think you have the wrong gentleman."

Rather started to walk around him and, as a second man hurried over, the first punched Rather in the jaw, under the left ear. Then the two men tried to pull him to the ground, but Rather was able to wrest free and started running. The men chased him, and when Rather ducked into the lobby of 1075 Park Avenue, they followed him. While doorman Danny Kavanaugh watched, startled, the men grabbed Rather and wrestled him to the floor, repeating the question over and over as they punched him and kicked him in the back.

Running to the intercom, Kavanaugh called building superintendent Bob Sestak for help. When the superintendent arrived, he and Kavanaugh ran over to help Rather and the assailants fled.

"Dan was in a lot of pain," Sestak recalled. "He told me who he was, but he was difficult to understand because he was having trouble talking."

Holding his side, Rather let Sestak lead him to a couch. When Sestak was sure the newsman was okay, he called police. A squad car took Rather to Lenox

Hill Hospital, where he was treated for cuts and
bruises to his chest and back, and to the left side of
his face.

To this day, Rather has no idea what the two men
wanted. A week before, he'd entered his summer
house in East Hampton, Long Island, as it was in
the process of being burglarized. The robber had fled
empty-handed; had he been stalking Rather in New
York to pay him back?

Rather doubted that. He also didn't believe that it
was a sick prank. The attackers were not your average, unpolished muggers. He could only conclude that
it was a matter of mistaken identity. He'd been
dressed casually and was wearing glasses; apparently,
they thought he was someone else . . . luckily for
Kenneth.

After nursing his wounds at his apartment on Sunday, Rather was back at his desk on Monday night,
his face slightly bruised and swollen but his professionalism unshaken.

The next incident was worse.

Part of Rather's ongoing quest for excellence is
"doing what I can to maintain the integrity of the
news department." On September 11, 1987, Rather
was in Miami, covering Pope John Paul II's visit to
America. At 6:15, while Rather was getting set to
anchor the 6:30 broadcast of the evening news, he was
informed that CBS Sports was planning to stay with a
U.S. Open match between Steffi Graf and Lori
McNeil.

Angry, Rather phoned CBS News headquarters in
New York, and protested that the sports division had
no right to preempt the news for a semifinal tennis
match. Told to wait and see what happened, Rather

Dan Rather anchors the news on the Monday after his mugging. Note the cut under his left eye and swollen jaw on the left side of his face. (AP/Wide World)

said that if the match went over, CBS Sports would be responsible for filling the entire half hour: he had no intention of doing a truncated version of the news.

With that, Rather returned to his anchor desk, hoping to make the broadcast.

When 6:30 rolled around, the match still hadn't ended and the network stayed with the tournament.

Assuming the sports division would, in fact, fill the half hour, Rather pulled off his microphone, left the desk, and headed for the phones. Meanwhile, the match ended at 6:32; CBS Sports signed off quickly, and by 6:33 the airwaves had been turned over to *The CBS Evening News*. Only they were in no position to broadcast: Rather could not be found.

The Miami bureau was frantic. There were a total of four minutes of taped segments they could show, but the producer in New York rejected going to those for fear that there would be no one to read the live material when they came back. Instead, affiliates got nothing from CBS News. Many aired "Please Stand By" placards; other aired blackness.

Finally, someone located Rather. When informed that the network was black, he felt as though he'd been punched in the gut. He hurried to the desk and began the broadcast. It was now 6:39, and though Rather's intentions had been pure, many affiliates believed he'd acted irresponsibly. The print media gave him a rough time, with headlines like "Vanishin' Dan" and "A Black Eye for CBS."

The truth is, although Rather *was* annoyed, he would never have left his post if he thought the sports division were going to leave the air. It was a misunderstanding, but opponents of the newsman used it as an example that he was becoming, in his own words, "unglued."

But the worst setback of all occurred on January 26, 1988. With the presidential primaries about to begin, and the Iowa caucuses looming—with Vice-President George Bush trailing Senator Robert Dole in the polls—the vice president was eager to escape his "wimp" image. Thus, he agreed to a live interview with Rather on *The CBS Evening News*. The Bush camp insists that Rather had promised not to discuss the ongoing Iran-Contra investigations; Rather claims to have agreed to no such preconditions. And he wouldn't have, either. Rather didn't build his White House reputation on timidity, and he wasn't about to develop a yellow streak now.

The White House knew this, and Bush was ready. When Rather asked about the affair, the well-rehearsed vice president replied, "It's not fair to judge my career by a rehash of Iran. How would you like it if I judged your career by those seven minutes when you walked off the set in New York?"

This, from a president whose inability to ad-lib is legendary.

Bush had set a trap for the man who was regarded as the personification of the East Coast Liberal Press, and Rather had walked into it.

Never mind that the vice president managed to make two erronous statements in one sentence (it was six minutes, and the location was not New York). Never mind that Rather wasn't running for office, and Bush was. The bottom line was that Bush looked resolute, while Rather looked pushy. Especially when, clearly bugged by the ambush, Rather cut the vice president off while Bush was in the process of evading a question: asked if he would be willing to hold a press conference before the February 8 caucuses, the vice president started talking about how he'd held "eighty-six news conferences since March and—"

"I gather," Rather interrupted, "that the answer is no. Thank you very much for being with us, Mr. Vice President."

Polls conducted by *Time* magazine and *Newsweek*

said, respectively, that Bush had won the showdown or that it was a draw. Ironically, a majority of people thought Rather was right to ask the question, and a whopping 79 percent felt Bush was not telling everything he knew about the affair.

But that didn't matter. Rather was perceived as disrespectful and out of line. Almost at once, "Dump Dan" bumper stickers were advertised on the front page of *The New York Times*, followed by another ad that asked, "Are you mad at Dan Rather?" and gave a toll-free number to phone. Callers got a recording that provided Rather's direct line at CBS, and were urged to call and complain about his lack of patriotism. In this instance, at least, Rather managed to one-up his detractors while maintaining a semblance of good humor: anyone who called the office that day also got a recording—of *The Star Spangled Banner*.

Rather has managed to stay out of the news since then. Ratings of the show have not improved, due in large part to the ongoing popularity of Jennings, but also because a handful of affiliates have put more bankable game shows on in the 6:30 or 7:00 time period, shifting Rather to different time slots when there are fewer televisions in use.

Nonetheless, his spirits are good. And, in his articulate way, he sums up the challenges facing all newscasters on TV today.

"We're all going through a period of cyclonic changes. *Cataclysmic* changes. All of us here at CBS and also the people at NBC, ABC, and CNN, are operating in a more hostile environment than ever before. Everything tests our effectiveness and resources, from takeovers to management changes to downsizing to viewership declining to more things being available on TV—it's all in flux.

"Look at NBC, which is owned by General Electric, one of the largest defense contractors in the world. What is the role of the news division in a global conglomerate like that? I don't know, and I'm not sure *they* know—but it's no small challenge to keep your objectivity and integrity in situations such as that."

Yet, what's most amazing is Rather's answer to the question, "If you could change one thing, or have any wish granted about your professional life, what would it be?"

Given all that's happened, one can't help but be surprised and moved when he answers without hesitation, "God give me another day of doing this job."